Book 5

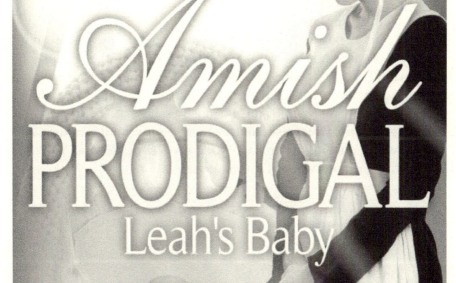

Amish PRODIGAL
Leah's Baby

ROSE DOSS

Amish Vows:
Amish Prodigal
By
Rose Doss

Cover images courtesy of period images & Canstockphoto
Cover by Joleene Naylor

Smashwords Edition

~∿~********~∿~

Dedicated to Dian McClain, Dian Simpson and Kay O'Brien. You are blessings to me.

~∿~********~∿~

Table of Contents

About the Author
Glossary   of   Amish   Terms

Chapter One

Leah
<u>Windber, Pennsylvania</u>

"What do you mean, we are not going to tell our *Eldre* about deciding to marry?" Leah echoed the question numbly, looking up from the pins she'd just slipped in to secure the waist of her skirt.

A gust of autumn wind shook the barn, making the flame inside their one lamp wiggle and dance. Hay dust filling her lungs, she waited for his response.

A flush ran up under Josiah's tanned face and he ducked his sandy blond head as his mouth firmed.

Staring at the *Mann* with whom she'd just promised to share her life, Leah felt her bare feet, numb against the rough floor boards. Confusion rioted through her and suddenly, she felt very cold.

"I just think," he responded in a tight voice, "that we should let my *Mamm* get to know you better."

Silence filled the barn for a moment before Leah said, "Josiah, you asked me to marry you and I've said yes."

"*Yah* and I want to marry you. I do. We just need to...to wait...a little while."

"Why?" She tried to keep her voice from rising. "My *Eldre* haven't met you, either, since we live in another town, but they will trust me to know I've found the right *Mann*!"

She deliberately took a breath, reassuring herself. He did love her. She knew it. His kisses showed his great love for her.

"Your *Mamm* has met me at the meetings and Sings," Leah reminded him. "She and I haven't spoken a lot, but we have met. Why should we not tell anyone about marrying? Of course, this is a private matter between our families. We wouldn't talk about it to others, but not tell our parents? Why?"

"My *Mamm*..." he paused, "can be difficult. I'm her only chick. Give her some time to get used to this."

"Get used to her grown son marrying? Have you—Have you even told her that we've been seeing one another?" The

1

appalling possibility that his mother didn't even know of her existence shook Leah. "Isn't that what *Gott* wants us to do? To choose a mate to share our lives and bear children?"

"*Neh*, I've not yet spoken with her about us and, *yah, Gott* does urge us to choose mates." Pulling on his jacket, Josiah didn't meet her eyes, "but it's just been my *Mamm* and me for such a long time. She's guarded and raised me since my *Daed* and *Bruder* died. She needs some time to get used to all this."

"How much time?" she demanded. One moment, she'd been in his arms, secure that she'd found the one *Mann* for her. Suddenly, she was shivering with an unnamed fear.

"I don't know." He lifted an unreadable face to her. She'd always been able to read Josiah before.

"Do you plan to invite me to your *Haus*? To tell her, at least, that we're courting?"

The fall season was upon them and she'd assumed they'd be husband and wife in a few weeks. Couples usually married in the cold seasons as the farms needed no attention. "I thought you would come to Mannheim with me to speak to my *Eldre*."

"I think we should wait," Josiah said finally, in a level voice. "We should keep meeting at the Sings and gradually let my *Mamm* get used to seeing us together. Then, after a while, I could invite you and several others to our *Haus*."

"For how long do we wait? Do you think Ada won't like me?" Leah reflected that his pretty *Mamm* often seemed to look through her with icy grey eyes. Maybe he was actually afraid Ada Miller wouldn't approve for some reason.

"It's not a matter of her not liking you. She just worries about me and wants the best for me."

Staring at him with gathering dismay, Leah blurted out, "Are you more worried about your *Mamm's* feelings than mine?"

"Of course not," he shot back, "but you could be reasonable about this.This is my *Mamm*. Women naturally wish their sons to marry a *Maedel* who will make them happy and share the load!"

"And you think your *Mamm* won't believe you'd be happy with me? She'll doubt that I will share your load," she spit out what seemed like the obvious conclusion, even though he didn't seem to want to say the words he clearly meant.

2

"Leah! My *Mamm* knows I haven't found my *Frau* among the *Maedels* here in Windber or on my *rumspringa*. Of course, she doesn't want me to be alone all my life. Be reasonable about this. I want to give her a chance to get to know you as I have."

Feeling herself soften a little at his plea, Leah wavered. Should she stay here in Windber, waiting until...? When?

"How long?" The words came out numbly, fear that she'd made a horrible mistake crowding up into her throat. "How long do you think we should wait?"

It was Josiah's turn to heave a gusty sigh. "I don't know exactly. How can I say? Of course, I will look for a *gut* time as soon as possible."

He reached over to pick up his broad-brimmed hat from where it hung on a stall door.

"But you can't say? Can't say we are to marry, or when you will feel your mother knows me well enough not to be upset that you've asked me to marry you? In a few weeks possibly?" Her words were toneless as her conviction grew that Josiah wasn't the *Mann* she'd believed him to be.

"Don't be like this," he said with irritation.

"Like what?" This was wrong and every part of herself knew it. Leah knew it.

"Irrational. Ridiculous."

He looked angry and, all the sudden, Leah was angry, too. "I tell you what, Josiah, why don't we forget this whole thing happened. You don't have anything to gently—eventually—break to your *Mamm* and I will also act as if you never asked me to marry."

"That's not what I meant, at all," Josiah insisted irritably, "and you know it."

"All I know," she said, picking up her jacket, "is that you and I spent an afternoon together that I wish only to forget."

With those words, she slipped her arms into the jacket and turned to leave the chilly barn.

Not in any of the moments it took her to do this did Josiah say anything. Finally, when her hand was on the barn door, he said irritably, "Don't be like this. If we are to be married, you can't just walk away."

3

"Only we aren't to be married…are we?" she shot back, longing for him to tell her she was wrong.

"Not right away!"

"You know very well that marriages take place in the fall—now—because of farm duties being lighter." Leah looked at him, standing in the vast barn. "So, if not this fall, then the next. Or the next. Or the next. I don't think you want to marry me."

"I do," Josiah's annoyed expression was stiff. "just not right now."

"*Neh*, you don't." As she walked away from the barn, alone in the dusk, tears rolled down Leah's face.

*

Leah
Mannheim, Pennsylvania
Eighteen Months Later:

Butterflies of excitement and dread in her stomach, Leah grasped the cool metal handle to open the door to *Onkle* Gideon's smithy, the spring air around her smelling of blooming plants and fresh beginnings.

She desperately needed a new beginning.

Dear Gott,

Thank You for being always with me. Even in my poor choices and my terrible struggle. I rely on Your strength now.

Gott understood why she'd never told anyone the identity of her son's father. *Gott* loved her and wouldn't want her to live as an *obligatory* wife. He'd also comforted her while she was in the cold, lonely *Englischer* world and convinced her to return home.

Yah. She'd had reasons for not telling Josiah when she knew a child was on the way, but she saw now that she should never have left her child. Even if she'd then thought that best for him.

Baby Eli was inside the 'smithy with her *Onkle* and Leah could hardly wait to see her child. She drew in a shuddering, hopeful breath. Her *Boppli* probably wouldn't know her now, since she'd been gone all these months. Lost in the *Englischer* world.

Leaving him had been so hard. She'd only been able to do it, believing he was better off without her.

Leah gulped in another breath, hoping desperately that she'd heard accurately *Gott's* direction to return. She prayed every day. Almost every moment.

She had so much for which to apologize. The church bishops still had to be met with to help her find her place again in this plain, simple Godly life.

Now, though, she had to get her sweet baby.

Down the muddy drive, several yards away, her *Mamm* waited in the buggy. Leah's hand trembled on the door handle. She knew her struggles had been painful to both her *Eldre*. She didn't know how, but she had to make all this up to Rachel and Mark Lapp.

Drawing in another deep breath, Leah lifted her chin and tried to quiet the butterflies in her stomach. It was time to stop running away and make a home for her little *Buwe*. Her long nights of prayer convinced her of this one thing. Leaving hadn't made anything right. She only hoped Eli remembered her.

With a gust of spring air helping her push open the door, Leah stepped into the shop.

Blinking as she stepped in from the light outside, the smell of fire and molten metal greeted her.

Standing at the far end of the building in front of his forge, *Onkle* Gideon turned toward her, hammer upraised.

The heavy hammer landed on the anvil with a faint thud as he stared at her, astonishment and joy in his face.

"Hello, *Onkle* Gideon." Leah's smile was tentative. "I'm back. Please, how is my sweet *Boppli*?"

*

Josiah
Windber

5

"*Mamm*," Josiah Miller said flatly, his hand on Ada's trim shoulder as his mother stood at the stove in the warm kitchen. "There will be no more wife-searching trips for me."

He hated having to say this to her so strongly, but she was bull-headed.

Ada reached a hand up to briefly cover his, throwing Josiah an understanding smile. "I understand. This is too stressful for you. I will go alone to scout out possibles next time. This wife-hunt has been hard. The trip to Mannheim wasn't fruitful."

His thoughts full of Leah, he tried and failed to push away the image of her sweet, beautiful laughing face.

Where was she?

The reason she'd given had made no sense.

"*Neh, Mamm.*" Josiah managed to say, "No more wife-hunting."

As if she hadn't heard him, his mother poured out coffee into a plain mug. "I'm also disappointed in Sapphira Schwartz's services. Hagar Hershberger just wasn't the right one for you. I guess it just goes to prove that using a beginner matchmaker doesn't pay off."

Reflecting that he was beginning to wonder if his *Mamm* thought any woman was right for him, Josiah went to stand by the fireplace that warmed the now-chilly morning air in the room.

"No, *Mamm*. That's not what I mean. Hagar seems like a fine woman."

His *Mamm* had followed him to the fireplace to hand him a mug and Josiah wrapped his hand around it. "What I mean is that you will not do wife-searching for me, at all. No more."

"What?" She stared at him.

Josiah knew he could no longer ignore the reality that he hadn't healed from the time with Leah, hadn't recovered from feeling as though his heart was ripped out. He still loved her. It was stupid of him, but he still loved her, even all this time later. There was no point in dragging a perfectly fine woman into it.

Josiah shouldn't have allowed his *Mamm* talk him into going with Sapphira Schwartz to Mannheim. If he hadn't known that was Leah's hometown, he might have had better motives in going there. His one furtive visit there last autumn after Leah left

Windber hadn't been fruitful. They'd just argued more, leaving him to slink home again.

No matter what he'd said, Leah hadn't heard his side of things.

Swallowing the angry lump in his throat, Josiah pinned a tight smile on his face as he glanced at his *Mamm*.

If anyone had a right to be mad about this mess, it was him, not Leah. She'd just left him. Slipped away before he knew it. Well, he'd known she was leaving the barn, of course, but not the area. The friends she'd stayed with had only said she'd had to return home suddenly.

He remembered having turned to stone when he heard she was gone.

Clearing his throat, Josiah said in a level voice, "I mean nothing against Sapphira Schwartz. She found Hagar, who was a very nice woman. She just wasn't the woman for me."

He couldn't imagine any other wife besides Leah...and that had gone so wrong.

Josiah turned to hold his mother's gaze. "Understand this, *Mamm*, you no longer need to concern yourself with finding me a wife."

Ada looked up from straightening a throw blanket over the back of the wooden settle. "Of course, this needs to be attended to, Josiah. *Gott* wants all to have the comfort and support of a mate. If not Hagar Hershberger, then we will search for the right woman. You are my son. I want you always to have what you need to best serve *Gott*. In this way, you will be happy."

Josiah glanced up at her with a tight, but not ungrateful smile. His mother loved him. The last year and a half had been harder than he imagined with long, sleepless nights of regret. He'd fallen completely for a charming *Maedel* for the first time in his life, a woman with whom he wanted to spend the rest of his life and she'd thrown his love back in his face.

Leah Lapp. She fit into his heart like she was made for him.

And then *BAM*! She was gone. Leah had been so passionate in her reaction that night and then later when he'd waylayed her near her home in Mannheim. Her demands were

7

unreasonable, given the situation, but he still ached with missing her.

Gott, keep her safe. Even though he was angry with her, he wanted Leah safe.

He forced a smile on his face now, looking at his *Mamm*. "Of course, you want the best for me, but this matter of finding a wife must be mine alone."

Ada Miller returned his look with a glance that told him she didn't like his prohibition. He glanced back at the dark liquid in his cup. It was okay that his *Mamm* didn't understand. He'd been her focus and priority since his *Daed* and *Bruder* died, but this was Josiah's business. She was just trying to be helpful, but he had to sort it out himself.

His *Mamm* was a fine-looking, well-kept woman who'd survived the hard years of her widowhood with a steadfast spirit. *Gott* wanted them to care for matters of the spirit, not the flesh, but some were more blessed in that area. And her outward appearance hadn't made Ada Miller's life easier.

Feeling his jaw firm, Josiah wrestled again with self-doubt as he took a sip from his mug.

Leah had been a blinding, bright revelation to him, a breath of air that warmed him through. Asking her to marry him had been as natural as breathing. He'd never known he could feel so strongly about a woman, but her refusal to be reasonable about his dealings with his *Mamm* was ridiculous and wrong. Didn't *Gott* command them to honor their parents?

A constricted, troubled breath left Josiah's chest. He needed to pray harder for *Gott* to take from him this angry ache in his chest.

*

Two days later, Josiah fanned himself with his wide brimmed hat, using the back of his hand to wipe the sweat off his forehead.

Even in September, the day was warmish as summer showed a last face.

8

"You know," offered his farm manager and friend, Luke, with a grin, "we aren't in a rush to pull out this old fence post this morning. You could work a little less hard."

Placing the hat back on his head, Josiah responded, "Yes? I told myself this post would come out easier."

Anything to drive away this ache in his chest for Leah. He had to get over her. He'd never met a *Maedel* like her, who laughed merrily and seemed so very cheerful. Never before found a woman he could see himself happily married to for the next fifty years...

But she'd left him.

"I guess I'm in the mood to work hard." His teeth gritted, Josiah again shoved against the resistant post.

"*Yah*." Luke's glance was thoughtful. "Hard work can be *gut*."

Tall grasses waved in the field around them as the early fall breeze blew on Josiah's heated back. "This part of the farm acreage has lain fallow for several years, you know, and it needed a new fence before the crops are planted for the new year."

"*Yah*. If I've learned anything from my advancing years," Luke said, taking advantage of being in his late forties, "it's that planning what a fence post or a woman will do is never a *gut* thing."

Josiah smiled then at the farm manager who'd become his good friend.

"Since you and your *Mamm* returned from your trip to Mannheim," Luke observed, "you've been even less talkative. Less so this whole year. Was the trip not fruitful?"

Not looking up from wrestling the stubborn fence post, Josiah said, "*Neh*. Not particularly. We met some nice people, though."

"I'm not sure whether Ada is disappointed or relieved you didn't come back with a wife."

Josiah paused to send his farm manager a questioning look.

"This was a trip to find you a wife, *Yah*?" The other *Mann* responded in a rueful tone, shrugging as he spoke. "Ada loves you and your *Mamm* is used to being the only woman in your life."

Firming his lips, Josiah asked, "Are not *Eldre* to love their *Kinner*?"

9

Luke nodded. "Of course, and since you're Ada's only *Kinner*, she worries about losing you. She's already lost her husband and her first born."

"That was a long time ago. She's dealt with it." Josiah went back to yanking at the fence post. "She wants the best for me and that is to have a *Frau* and *Kinner* of my own. I can say this with conviction, though, *Mamm* will do no more wife-hunting for me."

He felt Luke slide another glance his way. "Don't kid yourself that Ada has moved on from the trials of her widowhood. Your *Mamm's* loss was years ago, but she still fears, even now. Even years don't make some hurts and fears go away."

Using his shovel to chip dirt away from the foot of the post, he said, "Does *Mamm* look so very fearful to you?"

Luke laughed and then responded confidently, "*Neh*, she doesn't. Ada's just better than most at hiding her concerns."

Josiah rested his gaze on his friend. Luke had run the farm with him since he'd finished school, helping him gain his footing in the business when he was starting out, as a *Daed* would have. Wiry, lean, on the taller side and strong, the brown-haired farm manager had become his best friend, as well, despite the differences in their ages.

Still, he'd told Luke nothing about having proposed to and lost Leah. Some things were too private to talk about.

*

"I don't know what you and that *Mann* Luke have to speak of," Ada said later that day as she sat on the back porch of their *Haus* for supper. "You were out with him all day."

"*Mamm*," Josiah threw her an amused look before using a damp towel on his neck and arms, "Luke is our farm manager. He's also my *gut* friend. We talk of many things and we worked pulling out old fence posts all day."

His mother made a *hmmphing* sound in her throat.

Josiah laughed. "What? Do you suddenly have a problem with Luke? After all these years?"

10

Ada lifted her head to send him a speaking look. "Luke Fisher thinks a lot of himself. He's such a cocky know-it-all. Did not *Gott* tell us to be humble and plain?"

"*Yah*. He also told us to be kind to our fellowman," Josiah responded, laying the towel on the porch railing next to him.

He bent forward to press a kiss on the side of her face. "You know you don't mind Luke. He's always been a big help. Even when I was just a *dum Youngie*, right out of school."

Responding to his affection, Ada threw him a smile before saying, "I suppose he has helped you to learn to run the farm, as my own *Bruders* live so far away."

"Yes, they do." Josiah sank down to the porch planks next to her.

"This was a *gut* job for Luke, though, after his *Frau* died and his *Kinder* all married and moved away. He's done all right for himself."

Tired both in body and mind, Josiah could only smile mechanically. "You should give Luke a rest, *Mamm*. I don't know what I'd do without him."

Looking steadily out on the farmyard, he felt his mother's concerned gaze on him.

"You're weary," she observed. "You work too hard."

Not responding to this, Josiah said, "Luke is a good *Mann*. I am blessed."

"Perhaps," she responded in an absent voice. "He has been helpful. *Yah*, I can see how he's a *gut Mann*."

Josiah looked up at her. A fair woman, she'd aged far better than most, only a faint threading of gray in the hair under her white *Kapp*. He knew the bishops had urged her to marry after his *Daed* and *Bruder* died, but she wasn't a woman easy to push.

Deliberately, Josiah said, "I've gotten the feeling that Luke likes you and thinks you'd make him a *gut Frau*."

"Don't be ridiculous," she responded, easily dismissing the subject.

Not having the energy to push the subject further, Josiah subsided into silence. He knew his fatigue came from more than wrestling with old fence posts.... He missed Leah. It made no sense. He'd lived fine without her all these years, but he missed

11

the sound of her voice and the sweet smell of her. Her gentle touch on his arm.

Scowling, he lowered his angry, confused gaze to the porch planks, his thoughts swinging back to his mother and Luke. He had no right to meddle in his *Mamm* and Luke's business. He couldn't even stop grieving a *Maedel* who'd spurned his offer of marriage and stormed away…

He'd been *narrish* to go after her and even that had done no   good.

Chapter Two

Josiah
Windber

Several days later, Josiah sat in the Beiler's scrubbed home, trying to focus on the sermon.

At the front of the gathering, the deacon spoke of *Gott's* love and of the importance of caring for others. The speaker talked of having been cheated in buying a cow that was misrepresented and of when this was discovered after the fact, of praying for the seller. The man clearly needed *Gott* in his life.

Josiah only hoped he could have the same response in a similar situation.

As the words flowed over him, the familiarity of the gathering encircled Josiah in a comforting cradle. He'd sat through this kind of service every other week for the whole of his life. Having grown up here, he'd sat to the side in which ever home held that week's service, his friends around him. Often, they made googly eyes at whatever area where the *Maedels* sat.

The thought brought a piercing memory of the first time he'd seen Leah, here visiting friends in Windber. She'd sat primly in her clear blue plain dress, her black *Kapp* neat on her blonde hair and, it seemed, he'd lost his heart in that first glance. Of course, the impression hadn't been real.

They'd met at Sings in various homes and played games together with friends. He'd several times driven her back to her friends' *Haus* in his buggy. She'd captured him. Captured his heart. Then, they'd met privately, walking along a brook or stealing kisses as he drove her around in his buggy. It had been a private, secret part of his life. Something so intense he'd never talked to anyone of it.

With her sparkling eyes and witty, sometimes sharp tongue, she'd seemed like the *Maedel* he'd been seeking…

Josiah had thought he'd found the woman of his dreams. He'd felt for her what he'd never felt before with any *Maedel*.

Sitting now on the Beiler's hard chair with the sermon rolling over him, wedged between his broad neighbor and Jakob

Troyer, who lived several miles away, Josiah's mouth firmed, his face feeling tight. He'd been wrong about Leah Lapp. That was all. When it came right down to it—when he'd offered her his all, proposing they marry—she'd grown demanding and unsympathetic.

He'd planned to spend the rest of his life with her at his side, the *Mamm* to his *Kinner*, but no. Leah had turned crazy and unreasonable.

Of course, his *Mamm* was important to him! Even more than other men. After his *Daed* and *Bruder* died when Josiah was young, his mother had devoted her entire life to caring for him. Even when pressed to marry again and have other *Kinner*, she'd held his small self as her priority Despite her own horrific loss, she strained every part of herself to comfort him. A little *Buwe* couldn't have asked for a more devoted *Mamm*.

All he'd asked of Leah was that she give him a little time to break the news of their engagement to his mother in the best way and at the right time. His mother hadn't known anything of it and Josiah wanted to ease her into knowing. That was all. It had been him and his mother for so long. He'd felt so private in his growing attachment to Leah, his *Mamm* hardly knew her.

She wouldn't even give him a week or two.

Keep her safe, Gott.

All *Kinner* were responsible for their *Eldre* as they grew older, weren't they? His *Mamm* deserved his love and respect. After all, Gott had told them to honor their parents. His *Mamm* had wanted him to find just the right wife, as all *Mamms* did.

Maybe it had been cowardly of him to keep Leah to himself all the time he'd been falling for her. He just felt so…so perplexed by this gripping, all-consuming love.

Josiah swallowed and blinked, jerked back to his surroundings. The fellow church goer that set next to him seemed completely focused on the sermon and Josiah felt humbled for a moment.

He had to pull himself together. Leah had left him. He had to get a grip and move on. Much depended on him. His farm and the welfare of those who relied on it. Luke, too. It was Josiah's job to find a *Frau* and begin a *familye*.

14

Drawing in a deep breath, he fixed his eyes on the deacon, vowing to do as he should. This business of wife-getting and family-starting had been put off long enough. He'd always wanted to be a *Daed* and hold his wife's hand as they watched their *Kinner* grow. *Gott* knew and had decreed that this was the best for each *Mann*. Josiah had drifted along, not finding a *Maedel* to his liking before. No wonder his *Mamm* had taken it on herself to find one for him.

With a growing sense of the injustice toward Ada, he reminded himself that his *Mamm* had put her life on hold until he was big enough to take matters into his own hands. Well, he was able, now, and his mother deserved better than a son who didn't concern himself with her.

He needed a wife…and Ada needed a husband. It was time for him to stop pining for Leah and go on with life.

If he could…

*

Leah
Mannheim

Cuddling a squirming six-month-old Eli close before releasing him to sit up on the rug at her feet, Leah cleared her throat nervously. Her *Mamm* and *Daed* sat nearby, her *Daed* pushing a worn wooden pull toy Eli's way.

The cozy, familiar *Haus* that had been her home all her life seemed so wonderfully familiar, so welcoming. Leah ran her hand over the faded green fabric seat of the chair beneath her. It had probably been a dress skirt before. As *Gott* pointed them to the inner things, Leah knew a simple, plain life was preferred.

Leah sent up a prayer of thanks. All through the difficult times, He was by her side.

Outside, the sounds of her *Bruders*, Joel and Judah, could be heard as they walked past the window toward the barn.

Leah drew in a deep breath that carried the wonderful, homey scent of baking bread and the feeling of being home sank further into her bones.

15

"I know—I know I will regret every day not being here for Eli in the first months of his life," she finally said with resolution. "I was so lonely when I was away in the *Englischer* world. I know, also, that I have grieved you. I'm so sorry. So sorry."

Her *Mamm* reached out a hand to clasp Leah's knee strongly. With tears glistening in Rachel's eyes, she said, "We love you. We are very glad you're back."

Smiling at her, Leah said, her own eyes moist, "I have spoken to the Bishop. No matter what censure I face, I am returned and I want to join the church."

"Bishop Troyer has said you can do this?" Her *Daed* looked worried as he spoke.

Leaning over to straighten Eli, who had wobbled to one side, Leah responded. "We only talked the once, so far. As you, he said I was welcome to repent and make my peace with *Gott*. He believes the church will accept me."

Lifting her face, she said in a strained voice, "My *Onkle* Gideon said Eli and I will always have a home with him…but I hope… I pray you will let us live here with you and my *Geschwischder*."

After a moment—during which Leah felt her heart in her throat—her *Daed* said in a thick voice, "We also want this, *Dochder*."

Her *Mamm* quickly switching seats to hug her, Leah choked out, "You are such *gut*, loving *Eldre*. I know I have grieved you terribly."

Her *Daed's* smile was watery as he responded, "*Yah*, but you are worthy of all our concern, *Dochder*."

Rachel nodded, "You and Eli are always welcome."

"This is a great relief to me." Leah sniffled back her tears. "I know I have a way to go in my journey back to earning your faith."

Her *Daed* drew a breath. "Do you not think it's time to tell us about Eli's father? Does this *Mann* not care about his responsibilities?"

"Unless," her *Mamm* ventured, "he's an *Englischer*? You have only to tell us. It matters not in our love for you and Eli."

Looking suddenly back at her lap, Leah responded with difficulty. "I—I cannot talk of him. Please do not ask me."

16

When she lifted her head then, she saw the look that passed between her *Eldre*.

"Of course," her *Daed* said. "This is your decision."

*

"I hope you will both be comfortable in here." Later that evening, Leah's *Mamm* reached over to twitch the worn blue and white quilt on the bed. Leah had shared the bed with now eight-year-old Naomi since her little *Schweschder* had been old enough to sleep away from their *Mamm*.

"We thought since you will have the *Boppli* in your room, Naomi can share now with Anna." Rachel's words seemed to tremble.

Having been so caught up in her own remorse, Leah hadn't immediately noticed her mother's nervousness. She looked then at her mother with the startled thought that Rachel seemed to feel awkward. If anyone should feel awkward, Leah knew she'd earned that role.

Please, Gott. Please forgive me.

She knew that He did, but she struggled to follow *Gott's* example and forgive herself.

"The younger girls should have been sharing a room before, since they are similar ages and you are grown now, but Naomi never wanted to sleep without you by her side...." The older woman's words dwindled away.

"I guess she learned how to sleep without me, after I left," Leah said, her guilt and remorse giving her words a hard edge. They'd talked so long about her upcoming *rumspringa* in Windber with friends, but always with the assumption that she'd return here to marry some local boy and start a life after joining the church.

No one had been more surprised than her to fall so headlong into love with Josiah. For a moment, Leah stood with the echo of his name—his essence—in her head. She'd loved him, still loved him, despite his having so clearly chosen his mother over her...

"Anyway," Rachel hurried on to say, "we moved the cradle in here for Eli."

17

"Thank you." Leah looked blindly down at the now-blurry quilt, tears in her eyes. "I—I don't deserve the kindness you and *Daed* are showing me."

"Now, listen to me, Leah," her *Mamm* said in a stronger voice and she reached over to take hold of Leah's shoulder. "You are not only *Gott's Dochder*, your *Daed* and I love you. We don't know what happened in Windber and we've never pressed you to tell us—"

"*Neh*, not through all the months before I had Eli," Leah confirmed thickly.

"And the only reason your *Onkle* Gideon cared for the *Boppli* instead of your *Daed* and I was," her mother's voice clogged with tears, "was because we grieved you so!"

"I'm so sorry," Leah said again, starting to cry herself.

Rachel drew her in close for a hug. "But you are home now. We don't have to go to sleep wondering if you have enough food to eat or a place to sleep. You are home and we are very, very happy about this."

Later that evening as the *Haus* grew quiet around them, Leah glanced into the cradle to check on little Eli as he slept, his arm thrown over his head. The sides of the cradle blocked any cool drafts and her *Boppli* was safely tucked into a blanket sleeper.

As she watched Eli sleep, her heart swelled with love. How many nights had she cried herself to sleep, praying and praying he was alright and that he knew his *Mamm* had left out of love for him? Her prayers to *Gott*, though, had left her impressed that she should return to her home and her *Boppli*. No matter the mistakes she'd made, she loved the child and would care for him with her dying breath. For him, she'd willingly face her mistakes.

Maybe she'd been wrong in not telling Josiah about her pregnancy. Even when he'd shown up here in Mannheim. She hadn't been sure then, but she'd had some inkling.

Some would say she should have told him and she wasn't always sure any longer that she shouldn't have. She only knew she hated him—and, sadly, loved him—more than she should. It wasn't the way of her faith to hate anyone...but her heart still felt battered by Josiah. Since he'd so clearly chosen his mother over her—despite what had felt like their overwhelming love—she'd not thought he'd care or want to know about little Eli.

18

Even when drowning in a wave a guilt at keeping their son from his *Daed*, she'd never wavered in her conviction that *Gott* wanted the very best for her. Out of duty, Josiah would have insisted they marry if he knew of her pregnancy. Not that she would marry him, in those circumstances. *Gott* would not want her to be forced into an obligatory marriage.

She might still weep when she remembered Josiah's crooked smile or the little frown between his eyes when he pondered something. That didn't mean, however, that she should accept less than being fully loved.

*

Nervously pleating her apron in her hand, Leah stood just outside the henhouse on Hagar Hershberger's farm, peering through the wire netting.

"Hagar?"

The tall woman inside the coop turned around quickly, an egg in her hand.

She stared at Leah for a moment, not responding.

Wearing a faded workaday dress with a black *Kapp* on her blonde head, Hagar carefully placed the egg in her basket, looking up to send Leah a level smile. "*Goedemorgen*, Leah."

Given everything, her tepid response could be no surprise.

Around them, hens clucked contentedly, pecking at the grain scattered on the ground for them. Seeming a little stiff, Hagar walked over and pushed open the coop door to step out.

"I'm sorry to bother you at your work," Leah said in a low voice, glancing at the hens. "I had to come, though. I just wanted to thank you—to thank you for your excellent care for Eli. You've cared for him so well. You've truly been a God-send. Thank you so, so much."

Hagar eyed her without expression, saying evenly. "I hope I gave Eli what he needed. He's only a baby."

Unconscious of the drama going on above them, the hens scratched and pecked at the hen house dirt floor.

"*Yah*. A wonderful, innocent *Buwe*." Leah twisted her apron between unquiet hands, acutely conscious of her bad choices and drowning in the welter of her own emotions. The last year had been…beyond difficult, but that wasn't her baby's fault. "Eli seems very well cared for. Gideon has told me everything you did to help—"

"Eli," Hagar quickly inserted. "I tried to give Eli what he needed…and keep him out of the way of the big horses in Gideon's 'smithy."

"And you did an excellent job." Leah's trembling smile widened. "Gideon tells me he wouldn't have been able to keep watch over the baby while getting his work done, if it wasn't for you. *Denki. Denki* so much."

She'd never have thought she'd enter motherhood alone—a single woman with no loving mate. Leah swallowed hard. She'd prayed for *Gott's* forgiveness, He'd probably wearied of reassuring her she had this—if *Gott* could ever grow weary. She knew her actions led to grief on this earth. As long as she accepted His love and His salvation, *Gott* forgave her…she just didn't know how to forgive herself.

She sent Hagar a strained smile.

Over and over, she'd prayed her gratitude for her *Mamm*, her *Daed* and her *Onkle* Gideon. All the community actually. Although the unrepentant were shunned to protect others in the church, it was Leah's own consciousness of guilt that had led her to leave.

At first, she'd truly thought her son would do better without her there… She'd felt so worthless, so conscious of the wreck of her life. Then, it had pressed on her over the days and months that leaving Eli couldn't be best for him. At least, it wasn't for her.

She'd already left Jo— No. She would let herself think of him. It was a constant struggle.

Leah sent Hagar another smile.

"I want you to know, Hagar, that from now on, I will take *gut* care of my *Boppli*. I ran away—" She swallowed again against the lump in her throat. "I know I didn't handle things well, but I've come back home. Eli is not to suffer for my poor choices. I know now that *Gott* is with me and—and, with His help, I'll find a way."

"I'm sure you will." Hagar said this slowly, as if surprised to feel this way.

Leah and Hagar never had much contact before, as they were not of an age to interact much, and Leah had gone to visit relatives in Windber for her *rumspringa*.

Hagar drew a deep breath before saying, "Your *Onkle* always believed in you. I hope you know this."

"I do." Leah nodded. "And I will always be grateful. I was— I ran away. I was upset and afraid. I ran away and I know I could have lost Eli forever."

She gave a little shudder. "*Onkle* Gideon has saved me from this. Even when I—"

"He loves you," Hagar hurried to say, interrupting the girl. "He loves you very much."

"*Yah*, he does." On the third try Leah's smile was stronger. "He loves well, does Gideon. Very well."

"He does. He truly does," Hagar agreed, seeming oddly wistful for such a practical woman.

Chapter Three

Josiah
Windber

Two days later, Ada Miller smiled at Josiah as she tipped the coffee pot to fill his cup. "I think this time we might travel to Harleysville to find you a *Frau*. There's a bigger group of Amish there and our choices might be better."

His mouth pulling down, Josiah looked at his *Mamm*, saying with emphasis. "Neh."

Glancing up in inquiry, as if she hadn't heard him right, Ada said, "I just think a town like—"

"*Neh*," he interrupted her, his jaw tightening. Taking a moment to silently ask *Gott* for strength, he paused. Josiah knew his *Mamm* meant well, but the wound to his heart after losing Leah was still too fresh. He felt bad enough for having inflicted himself on Hagar Hershberger.

Ada frowned in apparent confusion. "Sapphira swears there are younger *Maedels* there that we can look at."

"Hagar's age wasn't an issue," Josiah said, Leah Lapp's evocative image springing to his mind, "and I told you there would be no more wife-hunting trips."

It made no sense. He loved Leah still, even though she'd shown herself to have no faith in him.

His *Mamm* shook her head wisely. "I know I said Sapphira wasn't a *gut* matchmaker this last time around, but I think it would be kind to give her another chance."

Getting up to head out to his work in the barn, he passed his empty coffee cup to his mother. He put his hand on her arm and met her gaze steadily when she looked over at him. "As I said, no more wife-hunting trips for me, *Mamm*. Not with Sapphira Swartz or any other matchmaker."

She looked confused. "You don't want to come along? You want me and Sapphira to look around first?"

"*Mamm*," he responded with an edge in his voice, feeling his temper slip, "*Neh*. I have told you and I meant it. You are not to seek a wife for me, at all. No trips of that sort, for me, for you or for Sapphira."

He'd already told his mother this. Although he knew Ada wanted the best for him, he was beginning to wonder if she knew how to listen.

"Well, "I wouldn't send Sapphira without one of us," Ada said, exasperation in her voice.

Josiah looked steadily into her face, his mouth straightening.

"Look, I know you are a strong-willed woman, *Mamm*. Heaven knows we'd have had a harder time surviving after *Daed* and Seth's accident, if you hadn't been—"

Her color heightened, she interrupted, "Josiah, we aren't talking about that."

"—but you must understand me in this, *Mamm*." He went on, trying to leach the anger out of his words. "No more wife-hunting. None. Not for me. Not for you or Sapphira, either. You are not to choose with whom I'll be happy. This is not a matter with which you need to concern yourself."

"*der Suh*," Ada said earnestly, "you will be happier with a *Frau* and *Kinner*. How I could I not want you happy?"

For a moment, Josiah wrestled with himself, unable to dismiss the possibility that he'd let a loving woman slip through his fingers in trying not to unsettle his mother. The mess tore at him still. How could he not have worried about the woman who'd born him and guided his early steps?

If Leah had only trusted him to sort out everything, if she'd just given him some time to deal with his sometimes difficult *Mamm*. He and Ada had faced the world alone together a long while. His mother didn't know Leah as he did. Ada had just needed a chance to absorb everything.

If only Leah would have been reasonable...

He drew a deep breath, saying with a tight smile, "You must trust me in this, *Mamm*. Trust me to find the right woman. Trust me to marry when it's the right time."

"*Gott* has urged us to be fruitful and multiply." She covered his hand with hers. "In this way, you will have the best life. We just have to find a *Maedel* to take the best care of you and the *Kinner* that will come along."

Josiah took his hand from under hers to reposition his broad-brimmed hat on his head. Drawing a deep breath as he acknowledged to himself that Leah might have been right in this one thing. His *Mamm* seemed determined to get involved on his personal business. Was she scared to build a life for herself?

"*Gott* wants this for me?" he asked in the same level tone. "*Kinner* and a mate to share my life?"

He tried not to sound bitter. It wasn't his *Mamm's* actions that had ended his engagement with Leah.

"*Yah*. Of course, He wants that." His mother smiled at him.

"Does He not want this for you, too?" He met her gaze. As Josiah had grown older, he'd wondered about her single state. Amish widows generally married again and went on build new families. Josiah remembered asking her for more siblings after his elder *Bruder* had died in the accident with his *Daed*.

Ada looked down quickly, settling a plain white towel over the kitchen hook nearby. "*Yah*, this is why He helped me find your Daed. Gott gifted us with you and your brother."

Not responding right away, Josiah shifted the suspender straps on his shoulders. "Remember when I was a small *Buwe*, *Mamm*? You told me after *Daed* and Seth died that this was not the work of *Gott*, but sometimes the world in which we live is harsh and filled with evil. You said, *Gott* did not take life, but gave it."

Drawing a breath, Ada nodded jerkily. "*Yah*. I remember."

"Then, if He wants us to marry and be fruitful, why did you never take another husband? If this is so right for me, why is it not so for you?"

His mother's face was expressionless when she responded to his question. "My time has passed, Josiah. I have met and lost my mate, had my *Kinner*. You still haven't yet started."

"I'll be out in the east field," he said, not replying directly to her statement.

"Fine, I know Luke will help."

Before closing the back door," he glanced back at his *Mamm*. "*Yah*, he will. He'd do more than help me, if you'd let him."

Descending the steps from the back porch and walking across to the barn, Josiah concluded slowly that he might need to

24

leave the farm for a short time. If the conversation with his mother showed him anything, it was clear that she held more tightly to his life than her own. His presence seemed to occupy his *Mamm's* whole mind. Maybe he needed to take a break to let *Gott's* breeze flow through his mother's heart.

To tell the truth, he felt stuck himself. Maybe he needed to get away himself.

Without question, Luke would look after things here. Since Josiah could remember, Luke Fisher had worked the farm alongside him, always providing insight and assistance to the orphaned Josiah.

Luke could look after the farm and his *Mamm* and…Josiah could go away for a while. Maybe heal this ache in his chest for Leah Lapp.

Walking through the barn with it's comforting scents of animals and hay, he went out the backside of the building, hiking through his fields to the focus of work this morning.

He wasn't sure where he'd go, if he did leave for a spell. His *rumspringa* had been spent innocently enough at a cousin's home some miles away. Thinking of his sharp-eyed cousin, Bart, as he walked along, and the large Schwartz *familye* in Sugarcreek, Josiah dismissed that option. He wanted to visit them all again soon, but not now.

In truth, he could only justify leaving the farm if he returned with a helpful skill.

Tramping across a pasture left fallow for the season, Josiah ran through all the possibilities, his mind stuttering to a stop as he considered…blacksmithing. Farm animals and buggy horses always needed shoeing.

Gideon Lapp, in Manheim, was a blacksmith.

Yah, his earliest association with Mannheim hadn't been *gut*, but Leah wasn't there any longer. At least, she hadn't been there when Josiah went to the town with his *Mamm* and the matchmaker.

He assumed she'd married and left Mannheim, but the probability so depressed him that he didn't like thinking about it.

His steps coming to a halt as well, Josiah mulled the option. It wasn't as if he were returning—had gone to that place with his *Mamm*—because Leah Lapp came from there. When he and his *Mamm* had visited Manheim with Sapphira Swartz, he'd seen or heard nothing of Leah.

Chasing after her wasn't an option. *Menner* didn't chase after *Maedels* who'd shown themselves to be uninterested... His jaw firming, he reflected that he'd done that once after Leah left Windber, he hadn't and wouldn't go there again to follow her.

Starting to again move slowly through the fallow field, Josiah pondered. Blacksmithing was a skill useful on a farm.

Gideon had never been anything, but nice and Hagar was certainly a kind woman. Just in her acknowledgement that they both deserved more than a lukewarm marriage, Hagar had proven herself to be a *gut* friend.

Feeling a scowl bracket his features, Josiah couldn't help thinking that he might have only a lukewarm marriage in his future. For a moment, he'd thought he'd found a golden heart, but events had proven otherwise and he had to get over Leah.

He had to. And he had to step back from his *Mamm*.

*

"I guess you could two have had cooler days to wrestle out those old fence posts. Maybe," Ada observed from where she stood by clothesline in the yard later that day. She threw a bed sheet over the line with a practiced flick of her wrist.

How many times had she put sheets out to dry?

Josiah's farm manager, Luke Fisherer, stood by the rain barrel at the corner of the Miller *Haus*. From the corner of her eye, she saw him drink deeply of the dipper of water, tipping his head back as if he enjoyed the liquid sliding down his throat.

Setting the dipper aside, Luke looked at her. "*Yah*. I suggested we wait for a more comfortable day to tackle the task, but that *Buwe* of yours was determined."

"He certainly is." She felt her mouth straighten as she stared at the clothes pin she shoved over the sheet to hold it in place. She just didn't know what to do about Josiah. "Is Josiah not going to help you with that?"

"*Neh*. He's checking on the work in the far field." Luke took another drink. "Josiah seems to have something weighing on his mind recently. Any idea what that might be?"

Not looking up from her task, she responded, "*Neh*. Maybe. I don't know."

She glanced over at the sturdy forty-year-old *Mann* when she said this. Luke had brown hair and hazel eyes that laughed even when she could see no joke, but he'd worked with Josiah when her young orphaned son needed someone to teach him how to handle everything. For that, she could only be grateful.

Cocking an eyebrow in amusement now, he said, "Well, which is it? *Neh*, maybe or you don't know?"

With a final smoothing down of the sheet hanging on the line, Ada turned toward him. Bursting into speech, she declared, "I just want Josiah to be happy, no matter what my sister Judith says."

Luke waited, as if he knew she was burning after her sister's statement. "And what did Judith say?"

Ada did respond for a few moments.

"It's silly!" she snapped finally, remembering Judith's critical words.

"*Yah*?"

"Of course! I want the best for him! I am his *Mamm*, after all!" She crossed over to plop down on a flat tree stump, a troubled frown to descend onto her face.

Luke scratched at the back of his neck, lounging over to lean on a fence post near her.

Usually, she was pretty *gut* at keeping her troubles off her face, but she knew Luke loved Josiah like a son. Despite her son's and Judith's suggestion that Luke had a romantic interest in her, she felt comfortable talking to him of Josiah.

"That's the only reason I set up the wife-finding trips to other settlements, no matter what my *Schweschder* says." Ada looked up to insist, "It's certainly the only reason I contacted the services of Sapphira Schwartz. I wasn't even sure using a matchmaker was the best for Josiah."

With a barely smothered smile, Luke said, "*Neh*. It doesn't seem like his way of doing things."

27

"Well, maybe not," she said in an exasperated tone, "but the *Maedels* in this town are certainly not suitable. How else was he to find a *Frau*?"

"I think we have some nice girls living in Windber." Luke's tone was mild.

"Of course, we do," Ada responded sharply. "I just mean that none of them are right for Josiah. None of them love him. Not that they wouldn't be glad to marry a husband with a rich farm that could provide amply."

She nodded, her mouth twisting from the sour thought of her son dealing with such falsity.

"And you are the one to decide who best suits Josiah?" Luke ventured.

"I didn't mean that." She got off the stump, recognizing the defensive note in her words.

"But that's what Judith thinks?"

"It's not that I don't trust Josiah to make the best choice, Luke. I just want him to have a choice! I don't think *Gott* intended us to be limited to choosing mates from only those around us, that's all."

"You're not choosing a mate, at all, Ada. I mean, you're still unmarried yourself."

Looking over at him quickly, Ada snapped, "We weren't talking about me…although Judith said the same."

"Maybe we should be talking about you, then," Luke said irritably. "Judith probably agrees with me that you might be less concerned about Josiah's marriage possibilities, if you had a husband yourself."

"Then you're both silly!" she responded with crisp words. "What can my situation have to do with Josiah finding a *Frau*?"

Luke went on as if she hadn't spoken. "If you really planned to leave the wife-choosing up to Josiah, why not send him out by himself to visit other towns. Let him go alone or with a friend. And why hire a matchmaker?"

Turning abruptly to Luke, she said, "Of course, he's to choose, but that doesn't mean I have no concern in the matter. He's been my greatest concern all these years, Luke. How could I not have an opinion about who can best meet his needs?"

"*Yah*," he responded, his voice more dry than usual. "Maybe that's been too much of a concern to him. He may need to think less about your opinion, in this matter, and more about his own. I'm sure your *Schweschder* agrees."

Having said that, he splashed a dipper of water on his face.

Ada stared at the lean, compact *Mann* in front of her who was remarkable primarily in his fun-loving, joking spirit. That was if you didn't count the wide shoulders made more evident by his now-wet shirt.

Beads of water rolled down his strong throat... Wiry and strong, he had a faint scar on his chin from a childhood accident.

"Maybe you should let Josiah find his own wife and get yourself a husband," Luke snapped.

Over the years of his working with her son, she'd come to know Luke very well. He was a *Mann* of character for all his usual playfulness. She would have welcomed some of his lighthearted banter now, Ada thought, a little huffily. He had no reason to be *sauer* now.

This worry she felt for Josiah could not be unknown to him. Luke had had two wives die young and he could, therefore, understand some of the loss she and Josiah had faced. Luke had raised his four grown, married *Dochders* with the support of his family and their community.

"I have to get back to the fields," he said, turning away.

Ruffled from their interchange, Ada watched him leave. Were Luke and Judith right? Was she part of the reason Josiah hadn't found a *Frau*?

*

"Your *Mamm* is a *verhaddelt* woman!" Luke snapped out of the blue later that afternoon, as Josiah shoved against another recalcitrant fence post.

Glancing over at his friend, he responded to Luke's outburst with a faint, startled smile. Luke was normally so *gut* humored, it was unusual for him to sound this irritated.

"I know *Mamm* can be a handful," Josiah responded in a level voice. "How is she mixed up?"

29

Luke thrust his shovel sharply into the dirt at the base of the fence post. "She says she's all worried about you finding the right *Frau*, but she doesn't see anything to be concerned with her own single state."

He snorted. "Wife-finding trips."

"What do you know of this? She told you she's worried? She actually said she's worried about me not being married?" Josiah cast his farm manager a sideways look. Had Luke and Ada even crossed paths that day? He'd been so lost in his own thoughts, he hadn't noticed them talking. "That she is concerned I don't have a wife?"

"*Yah*!" Luke jabbed again at the dirt around the base of the post. "We talked of it just now when I was at the *Haus* getting a drink of water."

Shoving harder at the fence post without responding to this, Josiah was aware of an irrational sense of success in his chest. He hadn't done many things right, but Ada's response to their conversation was encouraging, even if worrying her wasn't his goal.

His *Mamm* was a contained woman. If she'd spoken of this topic to Luke, she might just have heard Josiah this morning.

Ignoring the sluggish cycling of his own thoughts, Josiah looked again at Luke. "Something about this irritates you? Is my *Mamm's* single state a concern of yours?"

Working side by side on the farm since orphaned Josiah had left school at fourteen, Luke had been his guide and mentor.

The older *Mann* looked over at him. "I've worked with you, helped on this farm, for a long time."

"*Yah.*"

Josiah studied Luke's flushed face, his suspicion of the *Mann's* interest in Ada growing. Was Luke romantically interested in his *Mamm*? It certainly seemed that way. More, even than he'd realized. Had he been so consumed with his own troubles that he missed the *Mann's* interest in Ada? Of course, they were both single...and of a similar age.

Truthfully, he'd never really given his *Mamm's* or Luke's romantic lives a lot of thought. Not until recently. They'd just been there beside him all his life as he tried to learn all he could to take on the farm left to him when his *Daed* and Seth had died.

30

In the manner of *Kinder*, it hadn't seemed important or seemly to consider the romantic lives of his elders.

And then…then he'd fallen into what had become the mess with Leah and he really hadn't thought about much besides her since. To his own frustration.

He had to move on.

"It just seems," Luke said, with more force than he naturally spoke, "that addressing our own lives is more important than worrying about others. Even if it is your own child. Isn't that what *Gott* recommends to us?"

"*Yah*," Josiah said slowly. "We are to concern ourselves with our own actions."

On the other side of the post, Luke frowned at the dirt under his shovel tip.

"Luke?" He ventured, "Why have you not married again? You speak of my *Mamm*, but you've not taken a wife yourself."

"How could I concern myself with that," Luke snapped. "I was helping Ada and you with the farm and then teaching you to run the place."

Having let himself finally see his friend's attachment, Josiah wondered that he had not noticed the attraction vibrating between them all this time. Luke and Ada. Joined in the raising of his orphaned self. Both alone because of the deaths of their mates.

Intrusiveness was unacceptable, but were they not, he wondered, to act in a manner to aid *Gott's* children? All reliance was placed on *Gott*, but… Had he somehow been a hindrance to Luke and his *Mamm*?

Maybe his leaving the farm for a time would be *gut* for all…

*

Leah
Mannheim

"Drat!" Hoisting baby Eli more securely on her hip a week later, Leah worked to disentangle the briars holding her skirt. The day was bright, sun dappling down through the trees.

31

The scent of dampness and cool forest floor filtered up to her as she attempted to free herself. Smiling to herself at the baby's gentle pats on her arm, Leah was deeply grateful *Gott* had sent her home.

She'd thought cutting through the wooded area would get them to *Onkle* Gideon's 'smithy more quickly and she'd been right. The shed that held his forge in Hagar Hershberger's backyard was visible through the trees. She hadn't, however, considered the under-brush in the heavily forested acres around the *Haus*.

"Just a minute, sweet *Buwe*," she murmured to the *Boppli* in her arms. "*Mamm's* tangled here."

Working at the thorns holding her long, navy skirt, she made another annoyed sound in her throat before Leah looked up— and her breath felt suspended at what she saw.

There, outside *Onkle* Gideon's 'smithy was a *Mann* standing next to a buggy. Even from this distance, she recognized him. His was the familiar figure who haunted her dreams and whose very face seemed burned into her brain…as well as being echoed in little Eli's.

Josiah.

Shrinking back instinctively into the shadow of the trees, Leah clutched Eli's warm little body close. She shifted further back, her heart thundering so hard in her chest that she felt sick.

The rattle of the buggy wheels must have been what caught her attention.

What was he doing here of all places?

Please, please, Gott, don't let him see me!

For a moment, a string of memories flashed through her mind. She and Josiah taking long walks in the lanes around Windber; Josiah's arms gentle around her; him holding her hands tight as he'd asked her to marry him. The ugly fight between them later that afternoon and then another when he'd followed her back to Mannheim.

The baby in her arm squeaked and she realized her grip on the child had tightened.

"It's all right, little *Boppli*," she murmured incoherently. "*Mamm's* here."

Why was Josiah in Mannheim? Had he found that she was here now? Had he come for her? The question raced through her thoughts. Coming home to her *familye* and to *Gott*, she didn't need this complication now. She was trying to reestablish herself, to make this right.

But here he was.

Maybe he wasn't here to find her, at all. Gideon had said Josiah's matchmaker had tried to arrange a marriage between Hagar and Josiah before Hagar had realized she loved Gideon.

Her gaze resting on the 'smithy into which Josiah had disappeared, she gnawed on her lower lip.

Had he changed his mind about Hagar? Was Josiah here in hopes that he could somehow win Hagar away from Gideon? No, Leah remembered with a sour twist of her lips, that Hagar had remarked once on Josiah's frosty mother not liking Hagar, thinking her too old to marry the woman's precious son.

Josiah's *Mamm*. Leah swallowed. While she wasn't the mother-in-law Leah would have chosen, Josiah was the problem. He'd loved Leah so little that he'd wanted to keep her a secret. How he'd planned to work this out, she didn't know.

Shaking her head now with tears clouding her vision, she knew leaving Windber to come home was the best.

Of course, not betraying her upbringing and herself—not bringing her beloved Eli into this world without a *Daed*—would have been the best choice. Although she knew *Gott* forgave her many trespasses, she was still struggling to forgive herself. Swallowing against the thickness in her throat, Leah fought to stay calm, jiggling to comfort the baby.

She'd thought they'd marry, she and Josiah, that being with him that afternoon wasn't so big a risk since he'd asked her to be his wife.

Leah felt herself grow hard inside. She brushed a kiss against Eli's head and vowed to always remember the tough lessons she'd learned. She knew some would say she should have contacted Josiah to let him know she was with child, but she couldn't. Not after their horrible fight when he'd followed her to Mannheim.

He'd have insisted they marry then, even if he'd been forced to deal then with his mother. Only a scoundrel would do otherwise and Josiah wasn't a scoundrel. He'd have been obligated to marry her if he knew she carried his child. Forced.

She refused to be a wife by obligation,

No matter why Josiah was here, she'd not again carry her beloved child and herself down that rocky road.

Just then, little Eli gently smacked his chubby hand against her bare arm.

Leah looked at the 'smithy. "Eli, we haven't seen *Aenti* Hagar in several days. Let's go visit her."

Chapter Four

An hour later, Leah opened the 'smithy door and walked in. Josiah's buggy had just rolled out the drive.

"Hey, Nibling!" Gideon waved the huge hammer he held above a glowing hot horseshoe on the anvil, his broad arms bulging. "How are you and the *Boppli*?"

Her brawny *Onkle* glanced over. "Is he not with you?"

"Eli's in with Hagar. Why was your visitor here?" Her question shot out, tension in her words.

Gideon grinned, glancing toward the door. "Him? That was Josiah Miller, the matchmaker's suggestion for Hagar before she realized I'm the *Mann* for her."

Her *Onkle* smirked, clearly pleased with this.

"*Yah*. Why was he here?" she said without commenting on Gideon's engagement. "Is Josiah trying to woo Hagar again?"

Just as the question came out of her mouth, the 'smithy door opened and Josiah himself walked in.

"I forgot to ask when it would be *gut* for me to—"

As if startled into silence, his words came to a sudden halt. He and Leah stood staring at one another in shocked stillness.

Standing behind his anvil, Gideon looked back and forth between the two.

"Did you want something else?" he finally asked Josiah, a thread of amusement in his words.

Leah knew her glare was stony as Josiah stumbled again into speech. "My apologies. I thought you were still alone."

"This is my niece, Leah Lapp," the big man said with a grin. "Leah, as I was just telling you, this is Josiah Miller."

"Josiah Miller?" Her voice was hard and her insides where shaking so much she thought she might throw up. Anger pounded in her head at the confrontation and she wished she'd followed her impulse to run home when she'd first seen him here.

Their last ugly argument had taken place here when he followed her to Mannheim when she was still in doubt about being in the *familye* way. Back then, he'd caught her as she walked to the Bontreger's store and they'd picked up their quarrel as if not miles from the start.

Her stomach in knots, she remembered as if it were yesterday how he'd once again insisted their marriage wait until his *Mamm* was ready.

She swallowed against the rock in her throat now, saying with a hard bitterness in her voice, "I believe we may have met in Windber a while back. My *Onkle* was just telling me you came to Mannheim with your *Mamm* several months back to meet Hagar Hershberger."

"Leah?"

If she hadn't been so angry and upset herself, his numb response might have gratified her.

Josiah stared at her, unable to believe what his eyes told him.

Leah? His Leah, here in Gideon Lapp's 'smithy? He'd known she came from here—had found her and tried to make her see reason after she'd stormed away from Windber—.

He'd thought of her constantly when on his ill-fated wife-hunting trip to Mannheim with Sapphira Swartz and his *Mamm*. But he hadn't found her there. Not then.

And yet, here she was.

The sudden rush of joy that had swept over him initially receded, followed quickly—so quickly—by the remembrance of their last, harsh conversation so many months ago.

Feeling as if the ground had been pulled from under his feet, he took another hard breath. She'd walked out on him back then, and repudiated their agreement to marry when he followed her here.

Anger surged through Josiah with the memory.

She'd left him, when he'd just shared the most special, breathless, amazing moments with her... Left him all because he wouldn't do as she demanded. She selfishly wanted him to thrust aside his other responsibilities, to disregard his own *Mamm*.

Silence beat through the 'smithy for a few moments, Josiah and Leah seemingly locked in a staring battle while Gideon looked on.

"There is nothing for you here," Leah said finally, taking a short step toward him, aggression tinging her defensive words. "Hagar is to marry my *Onkle* Gideon."

36

Josiah flushed, saying with equal defensiveness, "I'm not here for Hagar! Hasn't Gideon told you? I'm here for another reason entirely. He's to teach me to be a blacksmith."

Leah swung a look back at Gideon who shrugged his broad shoulders. "He wants to learn. Of course, I will teach him. Do you have a problem with this, *Nibling*?"

Staring at him with fuming antagonism on her face, Leah then made a sound of frustrated anger in her throat, storming out of the 'smithy.

Josiah watched her go, his mouth tight. She had nothing to be so upset about, she was the one who ran out on him.

"To answer your question," Gideon said calmly, as if the heated moment between Josiah and Leah hadn't happened, "We can start tomorrow, if you'd like."

*

The bottom of his shoe striking the buggy running board, Josiah vaulted himself in his buggy. *Whew*! Leah here! Here in Mannheim! Actually here in Gideon Lapp's blacksmith shop?

Slapping the reins against the back of the buggy horse, Josiah set the buggy off, trotting away from Hagar Hershberger's farm, his head abuzz with it all.

Leah in Mannheim. Had she been here all the time? Even before?

There had been no sign of her at the church meetings when he was here with his Mamm before on their fruitless wife-finding trip with Sapphira Swartz.

But here she was.

Right where she'd been when he'd come after her. Right where she hadn't been when he came back with his *Mamm*. In all truth, he'd thought she'd be in Mannheim when he came wife-hunting. Maybe even hoped she'd be here...

Josiah had thought of her every day. Even now, over a year from the last he'd seen her, his head cluttered with replaying their argument beside the dusty road. With the wonderful connection between them before.

It was more than he'd ever believe possible...

37

And then she'd yelled at him, refused to understand his loyalty to his *Mamm*. Storming off like that into the dusk after she'd promised to spend her life as his *Frau*. After she'd so sweetly lain in his arms. Everything had seemed so right with the world.

He'd been thrilled. Leah was to be his wife. He loved her.

His hands tightening on the reins, Josiah was flooded with the thought that she had no right to be angry. It was Leah who'd stormed away that night, Leah who'd refused to hear him when he followed her to Mannheim all those months ago.

And now to accuse him of returning here to court Hagar Hershberger!

A short, harsh laugh escaped him. Hagar had nothing to do with his coming here to Gideon's shop. And he'd turned out to be Leah's *Onkle*! The irony of it bit into Josiah.

All his quiet searching for her had turned up nothing and now…here she was.

He'd come back to Mannheim because it was a distance from his farm and his *Mamm*. Ada needed a breather from trying to run his life. She needed to attend to her own life…and maybe to see Luke for the *Mann* he was.

Josiah needed a breather, too, although why he'd come back here, he wondered now. He'd come away from his farm—here to Gideon's shop—to get that distance from his mother and to get his head straight after losing Leah.

Looking back, coming here to her hometown of Mannheim probably wasn't the best idea.

She hadn't been here before, he was sure of it. Even though, he'd found her here before, she wasn't here when he'd come with Sapphira.

Only here she was. Gideon's *Nibling*.

It seemed as if *Gott* was playing a joke.

*

Later that afternoon, when she was absolutely sure Josiah wouldn't return, Leah slipped into Gideon's work shed, Eli perched on her hip. She didn't think she'd ever take for granted the feel of his chubby hand on her arm. Holding him just warmed her heart.

She could certainly use some warmth about now.

Closing the door behind them, she saw her *Onkle's* broad back as he bent to tend to a gray mare's shoes. Putting Eli down on the rag carpet near a chair in the section of the shop, still kept there for the *Boppli*, she sat down in the rocking chair, waiting for Gideon to finish.

Finally, he untied the horse and led the mare out to the small attached pen outside.

Gideon walked back into the 'smithy just as Leah gave her hand to Eli, who was now standing. He wobbled, but he stood, cruising along as he held her hand to balance himself.

"*Onkle*," she said in a tense voice without any preamble, "you must not mention to anyone that I have a *Boppli*."

Once she recognized she was in the *familye* way, she hadn't told Josiah about carrying his child. Without question, he would insist on her becoming his wife.

His obligatory wife. If Josiah had truly wanted to marry Leah, he would have. No matter what. He'd not have hesitated to tell his *Mamm* they were to marry. He'd never have put Ada Miller ahead of them.

Feeling everything in her stiffen, Leah looked at her *Onkle*. She'd never marry a *Mann* obliged to take her. She knew *Gott* loved her and wanted her to feel loved in her marriage.

"What?" Gideon looked up in surprise from where he'd also given Eli a finger to hold. "What do you mean, not tell him you have a son? And why should I not teach Josiah Miller to shoe horses?"

"You must not tell anyone that I have a *Boppli*!" she repeated, ignoring his last question.

"Ummm." He glanced up with a comical expression. "Sweet *Nibling*, I think it's known that you have a child."

Leah looked down at the 'smithy floor, her mouth set in a tight line. "Not to those who have only recently come into our town."

"Like Josiah Miller?" The thread of amusement was back in Gideon's voice. "What's with you and him?"

39

She wasn't ready—and probably wouldn't ever be—to tell anyone that.

"He tried to steal Hagar from you. Of course, I am suspicious of him. I do not see how you aren't."

Gideon laughed heartily. "Hagar loves me. Josiah's no threat to that."

"How long is he to be here anyway? How long will this take?"

"Some months, I suppose," Gideon responded with a shrug. "Long enough to learn the basics of blacksmithing. Why? You don't want Josiah to know you have a child? I can understand why you might still feel others will look down on you, but Josiah doesn't even know you have no husband."

Glancing up swiftly, she said, "Perhaps not now, but he will likely notice this when he comes to meetings and sees me with no *Mann*. That and I wear a black *Kapp*. Anyone can see that I'm not married."

She fell silent a moment. *Please, Gott! Please help me know what to do!*

"Maybe he won't notice? There are a lot of people at services."

Her *Onkle's* voice was kind in his attempt to comfort her. She knew he couldn't understand why she was so upset.

Thinking furiously, Leah blurted out, "Of course, I could be a widow for all he knows!"

Breaking into laughter, her Onkle chided, "If that were so, I'd hardly think you'd be so excited about it. Your poor deceased imaginary husband! And you wouldn't wear a *Maedel's Kapp*."

With little Eli tugging at her hand, she stood to follow him as he cruised along the little fence Gideon had erected to keep him safe from the 'smithy.

"*Nibling*," Gideon teased. "You might want to reconsider keeping this *Mann* as an enemy. Josiah has no *Frau* and he has a farm of his own, from what Sapphira told Hagar. He could make you a *gut* husband."

Feeling herself flush, she said with vehemence, "No! No."

"*Nibling*," her *Onkle* said, reaching out to take the unstable *Boppli's* hand, "you must forgive yourself and not live in regret. I cannot imagine a situation in which I will have to say anything directly about Eli's *Daed*, but do not fear that I will tell any secrets or say anything that is your business to say."

"*Denki*," Leah responded, feeling his promise gave her room to breathe, "I just wish Josiah Miller found someone in Windber to teach him 'smithing.'"

Bending to kneel to catch her teetering son, she tried to ignore Gideon's puzzled glance.

*

The dark green late summer grass shushed softly under Leah's feet as she came up to the Glick *Haus* a week later, others around her hurrying inside to find seats. Her *Mamm* beside her, Leah balanced Eli on her hip, praying for strength.

She knew Josiah would come to the service. As a rule-following, *Gott*-loving *Mann*, he never missed church services.

Maybe he would think Eli was her little *Bruder*. *Mamm* was still young.

"Let us find a spot near a window," Rachel Lapp said, seemingly unconscious of the tension holding Leah's body tight. There was no reason why she should have known as Leah hadn't told her *Mamm* or *Daed* that her *Boppli's* father would be at the service.

"Dadadada," Eli babbled, as if he somehow knew who they'd see in the *Haus*.

Jiggling the *Boppli* a little, she reminded herself that her son was just exploring speech, trying to keep her agitation off her face. This had always been difficult for Leah, her *Daed* having said more than once that she was as easy to read as a book.

"Come," said *Onkle* Gideon, reaching out for Eli as he and Hagar came up beside her, "we need to get seats, as many have been able to attend this morning."

"It's to be expected," Hagar commented, making the *Boppli* chuckle as she tickled under his chin, "with the summer crop harvested and most of the fall planting done, most are free."

Dumbly releasing her child into Gideon's arms, Leah stiffened as she saw that Josiah followed behind Hagar.

41

Knowing her face reflected the annoyance she felt—mostly at the stupid gladness that sprang into her stomach at the sight of him—Leah reminded herself Josiah was now the enemy.

She tried to school her features. Of course, he was here.

All those long walks they'd taken along wooded lanes, she'd come to know very well the *Mann* with whom she'd wanted to spend the rest of her life. His tender kisses...

Having paused now beside elderly *Frau* Lehman, Josiah offered the old woman his steady arm.

Everything about Josiah was steady, the thought streaked through her head, except the part in the Bible where *Gott* said to leave your parents when you married.

Her mouth firming, she turned away from the sight of his kindness to the elderly. No matter how caring and gentle he seemed, Leah hoped the *Maedel* he eventually married would be fine with standing in line behind Ada Miller. Josiah had made it clear his *Mamm* came first and always would.

Leah turned, retrieved her child from Gideon. She had to stop focusing on Josiah Miller if she was ever to kick him out of her heart. Let him think what he liked. He couldn't prove Eli was his.

If she had to, she'd lie through her teeth. No matter what, she was determined not to be a wife he married out of obligation.

"*Goedemorgen*, Leah Lapp."

A shiver streaked up her spine, as if even her body responded to the sound of Josiah's voice.

Only turning her head halfway toward him, she kept any tremble out of her response. "*Goedemorgen*."

She stepped up her pace, heading toward the *Haus*, but he walked beside her easily.

With him clutching her arm as she held her *Boppli* on her hip, Eli decided then to gurgle in laughter before blowing a sputtering raspberry.

Her son had recently learned a new sound.

Josiah laughed as she momentarily cast her eyes up in frustration.

Her side vision reported that he reached out to touch Eli's hand. "*Yah*, what a *wunderbaar Boppli* you are."

Overcome with the urge to explain that this was not her son, but her *Bruder*, Leah pressed her lips together. She wouldn't repudiate Eli. Besides, the statement would only make her sound guilty.

Still not looking at him directly, Leah said in a strangled voice, "We must go in to find a seat."

"*Yah*, of course," he responded.

Quickening her steps, she caught up with her *Mamm*, sending up a prayer of thanks. With *Gott's* help, she at least hadn't messed that up too badly.

Her *Onkle* Gideon appeared next to her as Hagar moved to find a seat in the row ahead of them. "I saw you speaking to Josiah just now."

"*Yah*." She knew her response was terse, but Leah felt unable to say more.

"It's kind of you to welcome the stranger." Gideon looked at her as if he had more to say.

She knew from past experiences that Gideon was unusually sensitive to feelings and had definitely picked up on the chaos and anger she felt with Josiah. Not liking to disappoint him, Leah forced a smile onto her face. "*Yah*. Of course we want to be welcoming."

If she told her *Onkle* and *Eldre* who Josiah was, she knew they'd be on her side instantly. That certainly would be the end of him learning 'smithing from Gideon.

Still, she said nothing, her secret feeling frozen inside her chest. It didn't make sense, but she just couldn't talk about her dealings with Josiah.

The service that followed was long and comforting. Leah jiggled Eli on her knee, rigidly refusing to look in Josiah's direction. She was here where she belonged amid all her *familye* and friends and that gave her a wonderful, warm feeling.

Kate and little Elizabeth sat nearby and, in another room that opened onto the Glick living area, were Lydia Stoltzfus and her *Boppli*. Leah suspected Lydia's husband, Daniel, had given his *Frau* his seat. Looking around, Leah saw many life-long friends. Kind folk who'd forgiven her lapse more easily than did she.

Leah had prayed for forgiveness many times and believed *Gott* forgave her sins, but she had a hard time forgiving herself. As

43

if she somehow had higher requirements than *Gott*. It didn't make sense, but she still felt horrible about it all. She knew better. More reason not to let herself see Josiah kindly.

Her *Mamm* and her *Schweschder*, Anna, took turns holding the *Boppli* and when Eli grew fussy, Leah carried him outside for a few moments.

Soon, the final prayers were spoken and Leah left Eli with Rachel to hurry to the kitchen to help Kate with the meal. She liked cooking, as did her friend, and this part of feeding her loved ones always gave her pleasure.

After their meal was finished, clusters of people stood around visiting. Even with the summer planting long done, there was much to do on farms. Most worked so hard they had little time for visiting until the cold fall winds blew in. Sunday services were as much social occasion as religious ones.

As the day grew later, families hurried home for evening chores, leaving their *Youngies* behind for the Sing that was to follow.

Sitting between Anna Lehman and Abigail Hochstetler at a table peeling potatoes and chopping fruit for the meal, Leah felt again the happy rightness of being home again.

"Did you see that new *Mann*—Josiah—with Gideon?" Abigail giggled. "I understand he's working with Gideon to learn blackmithing. He's very nice."

"You think all boys are nice," Anna responded in a teasing voice. "Besides he's too old for you."

"Not necessarily," Abigail asserted with the eager silliness of a fifteen-year-old. "If Hagar Hershberger and Gideon Lapp can marry, I don't think actual age matters."

"You are such a giddy *Maedel*," Anna responded. "You don't know anything about him."

"Lower your voices, please." Leah said in a quiet voice, feeling herself grow pink as Josiah walked past with Gideon.

Abigail dissolved into a string of giggles as the two *Menner* went by.

"The cornerball game is set up over here," Gideon's voice drifted to them. "You don't have to play, you know, just because those two crazy *Youngies* asked."

Josiah smiled. "It's fine. I don't mind playing."

The sound of Josiah's level voice darkened Leah's blush to her frustration and she ducked her head look down into bowl of half-peeled potatoes in front of her.

"Okay," her *Onkle* chuckled, "but I warn you Judah and Reuben have yet to learn to be graceful in defeat."

Leah's hand ached from her grip on a potato.

The laugh she'd heard so sweetly in the past now rippled up her spine as Josiah responded. "What makes you think they'll lose?"

"I've seen you swing a hammer…"

The *Menner's* voices faded as they walked away.

Carefully placing a half-peeled stump of potato into her bowl, Leah only prayed the other two girls wouldn't notice the pile of creamy strips she'd let fall with the potato peel.

She had to get a grip on herself. Josiah was here, and while this was the first of their public meetings, Leah knew with a sinking sensation in her stomach that it wouldn't be the last.

Chapter Five

Ada
<u>Windber</u>

The August air cooler under trees, Ada sat under a tall oak to stitch the white Amish *Kapps* she sold to a middleman for the *Englischer* market. Stopping once in a while to fan herself, she sighed. She hated the heat and she missed her son. She wasn't sure what to do with herself without Josiah to care for. Making his dinner and washing his clothes. Since his *Daed* had died, she'd watched over him, but now he was gone off on his own.

Ada frowned at the delicate white fabric in her hand. She knew she could have made more money selling her *Kapps* at the roadside fruit and vegetable stand Esther Glick ran, but using a middleman meant year-round sales. Esther naturally only sold from her stand in the summer and fall.

"Aren't you melting in this heat?" she asked Luke Fisher, the older *Mann* who managed their farm.

The new clothesline he was installing was only a yard or two away, so she hardly had to raise her voice.

Thrusting his shovel again into the hole he dug, he then leaned on the handle, his lean, wiry body agile and powerful in the work.

He threw her a flashing grin in response to her question. "*Neh*. A little heat and hard work every now and then are *gut* for a *Mann*."

"I'm glad you think so," she commented. In the years of Josiah's young days, guiding and watching over him, Luke had been at her side. She'd naturally grown comfortable with him.

Luke forcefully thrust his shovel into the dirt to widen the hole on which he worked.

"I'd think," she commented, pausing again to fan herself, "that with Josiah gone off learning to blacksmith, you'd be overwhelmed with running the farm."

Pausing his hole digging, Luke smiled at her again. "Josiah is a thoughtful, considering *Mann*. Not a *lappich Buwe*. Josiah's not silly or a *Youngie* any longer. He carefully picked the time he's gone. You know the summer crops are in the ground and he plans to come back before the fall harvest. All there is to do now is water the crops and do some weeding."

Not responding, Ada let the organdy *Kapp* in her hands fall to her lap while her gaze brooded on the big red barn that housed hay bales and farm equipment.

After a few moments, he asked in his sympathetic way, "Are you okay?"

Luke leaned on his shovel again, giving her time to respond. Given his physical exertions, it made sense that he'd taken off his jacket for only his shirt and pants. The shirt was so sweaty, the fabric strained against his powerful arms as he'd dug into the dirt to make the hole.

"*Yah*. I'm fine, just down, I guess."

He looked at her thoughtfully.

"I was alone with the *Kinder* after Amity died," he commented, thrusting the shovel again into the dirt. "I realized after a year or so that it wasn't fair to the girls."

Ada lifted her gaze to meet his. "You never minded having only four daughters? No sons?"

Luke worked at clearing his hole. "Not of my body, but all my girls have now found *gut* husbands. Judith was helpful with that."

"She was your second *Frau*, wasn't she?"

"*Yah*. We had nearly six good years before she died, too."

Ada mulled over the unfairness of a *Mann* having two wives die young. "Did this not make you bitter? Two *Fraus* dying young? Did you not feel *Gott* had abandoned you?"

Pausing again with his hand braced on the shovel's wooden handle, Luke considered her words with a serious expression. "It was a bitter loss, both times, but Gott never said this world would be easy. I lost nothing like Job."

She thrust her needle into the snowy fabric in her hand. "Sometimes the Biblical stories seem far off."

"*Yah*." After several minutes pause, he said, "I know you grieve Seth and Abraham still."

A little startled by how his kind voice touched her, Ada bent her head to focus on the half-finished *Kapp* in her hands.

47

Blinking to clear suddenly damp eyes, she drew several deep breaths before smiling up at him.

"I've noticed you don't talk about them," he ventured. "Your dead son and your husband."

"*Neh*." She agreed, clearing her throat. "The accident happened long ago. Others have suffered losses and move on."

Drawing in and letting out another deep breath, she looked over to see he watched her with sympathetic eyes.

"The passing time doesn't mean you don't miss them any longer. Some say you never get over the loss of a child."

"No, one doesn't," she agreed in a stronger voice, "but I've chosen to attend to Josiah, to always watch over him."

"It is the work of a parent to watch over their *Kinder*," Luke commented. "It is also in the progress of life that our children become grown and we must let them arrange their own lives."

Ada gave him a hard look. "You are saying my son doesn't need to listen to the wisdom of his elders?"

"Of course not." Luke continued to scrape crumbling dirt out of the post hole. "Only that he is a *Mann* and must make his own choice regarding his mate. It is in the way of being a *Mann*."

"Josiah is strong." She tried not to sound defensive. "I've always wanted that. He makes his own decisions. He decided not to marry any of the local *Maedels*. He isn't under my thumb. He decided himself to go off and learn blacksmithing. That was his own idea."

"*Yah*."

"Are you saying I'm an interfering *Mamm*?" she demanded in a ruffled voice.

"*Neh*, not necessarily, but you must know he worries about you in this wife-choosing."

Bristling, she glared at Luke. "I don't ask that Josiah worry about me, but only that we both are comfortable with the *Maedel* he marries. Is that not reasonable? After all, I live here, too. I will naturally be affected by his marriage."

"That's another thing," Luke said, again chipping at the dirt in his hole. "It is common and in the natural way of things that you marry again and have other *Kinder*. Why have you not?"

48

If Luke wasn't such a longtime friend, Ada would have ignored his question, frosting him out with a cold look. As it was, he didn't even seem to think anything of what he'd said.

"Why haven't you married again?" He repeated, glancing at her casually.

The half-finished white *Kapp* sat ignored in her lap as her expression stiffened into a blankness she felt on her features.

"Are you not getting a little personal?" She turned her head to stare sightlessly at the barn. "Perhaps we should change the subject."

"I don't see why," Luke responded. "We are not strangers or distant acquaintances. You and I go far back. I came here shortly after my youngest *Dochder* married years back. If you and I can't speak openly, I don't know who can."

She swallowed. *Gott* help her, she could not do this. "Still, I cannot speak of this."

Ada got up out of her chair under the trees. "Are you hungry yet for lunch?"

"*Yah*," he said, tacitly accepting her change of subject. "I could eat."

"I'll have lunch ready in a moment," she promised, turning to head into the *Haus*.

As she did so, she could feel Luke watching her.

*

Josiah
Mannheim

A week later, Josiah brought the heavy hammer crashing down on the side of a glowing horseshoe that sat on the anvil.

Sitting nearby, Gideon chuckled. He wore a heavy leather apron like Josiah's, protection against scattered embers, watching Josiah's novice efforts with a smile. "It takes practice. You'll get the hang of it."

"I'm not so sure." Josiah's response was wry. "I feel like a clumsy *Hundli*."

49

Laughing, his teacher said, "We all do in the beginning. Is your arm aching?"

"Yah," he admitted, rubbing his right shoulder.

"Again, this is true of us all in the beginning of 'smithing."

"My *Daed* used to put shoes on his own horses," Josiah mentioned after a moment as he used prongs to shift the cooling shoe on the anvil. "I was young when he and my *Bruder* died in a carriage accident, but I remember being with him in a little shed he had on the side of our barn. His forge was small, but the smell is unforgettable."

"It is," Gideon agreed. "I learned blacksmithing from my Hagar's *Daed*. This is his forge."

He sighed heavily, sending Josiah a crooked smile. "I understand the smell bringing memories. Ben Hershberger was like a father to me."

They worked in silence then. Josiah pounding awkwardly at the cooling metal.

He looked up. "You and Hagar will be married this fall?"

"*Yah*." His grin dawned large. "It can't come soon enough for me. I don't know why it took us so long. She is such a blessing in my life."

Gideon stood in front of the forge, raking the embers into a pile in the center. His shirt sleeves rolled up to reveal powerful arms, he wore dark suspenders to hold up his pants. He was a big, highly-muscled *Mann*, his years of 'smithing clear.

Josiah didn't respond to his words, wondering if he'd ever again find a woman he loved as much as he had Leah. His feelings toward her now were a tangle of longing, defensive anger and something like an ache, that he didn't want to identify. He'd loved her like no other woman.

It still shook him that she'd apparently been here under his nose all the time. He'd have sworn she wasn't in Mannheim when he'd come on that wife-hunting trip with Sapphira Swartz. He'd looked for her at every gathering.

Gideon spoke almost as if he could hear the thoughts buzzing in Josiah's brain.

"I suppose Hagar and later, my *Bruder*, Mark's *Dochder*, Leah, have been the women most important to me. After my own

50

Mamm, of course." He grinned. "I just took a little longer to realize what Hagar meant to me."

He stepped back from the forge to stand the coal rake at the side. "Of course, she didn't make it easy, courting all those years ago with the wrong *Mann*. Leah, now, I always knew was special. I lived in Mark's *Haus* when Leah was small, you know."

"Did you?" Josiah didn't think Leah had mentioned to her *Onkle*—or anyone in Mannheim—that they'd become so close that he'd asked her to be his *Frau*. No one acted the least bit aware and he thought they would have. Amish thought it proud and intrusive to talk about couples, but they'd have shown some sign, surely.

"Your *Mamm* must be glad you'll be doing your own horse shoeing, like your *Daed*," Gideon commented from where he swept up the stall area before the next horse got there to be shod.

"I suppose," Josiah responded. He'd left Windber to put some distance between himself and his *Mamm*, not because he didn't feel her love, but because she had some difficulty in realizing he alone would choose his own *Frau*.

If he ever found a woman he loved like he'd loved Leah. Right now, he didn't feel hopeful about that.

Right now, he'd begun to wonder if he'd ever stop loving her.

*

Riding her bicycle to *Onkle* Gideon's a week later, Leah tipped her head back to catch the faint scent of autumn in the late summer wind. Patchwork pastures flew by as she cycled past, the crops ripening in the fields. All around her, the earth smelled of decayed manure and growing things, flourishing with green, yellow and red bounty. A gift of *Gott*. Brussel sprouts and different kinds of lettuces in fields next to those growing peppers and tomatoes.

A hole still burned in her chest for the life she'd thought to share with Josiah, but she knew she had many blessings. Turning her thoughts in this direction, Leah inhaled the scent of growing things, glad her route didn't take her past the King dairy farm. That had a different smell, altogether.

Pushing the pedals rhythmically, she balanced easily on the machine as she skimmed along the peaceful country lane, reflecting that her *Mamm* would have put Eli down for a nap by then. Her *Mamm* loved helping to care for Eli. Leah's child was not so much younger than her smallest *Bruder*, Reuben. Both Leah and Rachel felt they had some catching up to do with her little *Buwe* as her *Mamm* had grieved Leah's absence so much, all while she was gone, that Rachel hadn't cared for Eli herself.

Leah thanked *Gott* every day that *Onkle* Gideon and Hagar had given her the gift of watching out for Eli.

As she crested the hill before the Hershberger farm, Leah spied *Onkle* Gideon's 'smithy behind the Hershberger *Haus*. Even risking seeing Josiah, she couldn't not ever visit her *Onkle* and Hagar. She owed them too much and, besides, why should Josiah deprive her of this as well?

Glancing down quickly at the quilt in her bicycle basket, she was so glad she'd finished it in time for Gideon and Hagar's wedding.

Even in summer, a curl of smoke rose from the 'smithy chimney, as the forge would be used to heat the iron. Coasting her bicycle to a stop in front of the shop, she saw Josiah in the pen next to the building. With him was a horse she recognized as old Mr. Stoltzfus' buggy horse, Betsy.

The sides of Leah's mouth kicked up as she propped her bicycle against the wall and took the quilt from the basket. She turned her head, hearing scuffling from the pen behind her. Betsy was a wily old girl. Many a time, Mr. Stoltzfus complained about her ornery ways. Once he got the horse into the buggy shafts, she was a *gut* puller, but getting her to go in any certain direction up to that point was challenging. Mr. Stoltzfus had often said his Betsy would be the death of him.

The horse pen was located next to the building that housed the forge and a wider door opened to it to allow horses from the pen into the 'smithy to get new horseshoes. Apparently, Betsy needed a new set of shoes and Josiah had been given the job of getting her into the 'smithy.

Although Leah saw the *Mann* she'd loved so much look her way, Josiah said nothing, apparently focused on the horse.

In the small enclosure, he flapped his arms in what seemed like a move to send the rusty-red Betsy up to the building. Unmoved, the horse watched his gyrations with what appeared to be disdain on her long face.

For a moment, Leah stood watching Josiah as he first shooed the horse and then tried to capture Betsy's lead.

Normally calm and not easily flustered, his maneuvers with the mare brought a twitch to Leah's mouth. *Gott* forgive her, this was fun to watch. She wasn't used to seeing Josiah be other than calm and successful.

His attempts to capture Betsy clearly not working, Josiah strolled to the fence, glancing over his shoulder as if to measure how his casual act was being received. He stood by a post, resting a hand on the top rail, suddenly lunging at her when Betsy walked past.

Sadly for Josiah, the horse dodged, nimbly trotting away.

Leah burst into laughter, closing her mouth against the sound when she saw Josiah glance at her with annoyance on his face.

"She's a *Schaviut*, Betsy is," she called out, not completely able to banish the laughter from her words.

He cast her a level look and went back to where the horse stood in a corner of the pen. Betsy eyed him suspiciously, her ears perked.

Strolling slowly towards her, he stopped when the sorrel veered away a little, as if she were preparing to trot away. Josiah moved forward slowly, talking to her in a low, intimate voice that sent shivers over Leah.

She shrugged her shoulders a little, as if the action banished her reaction, still watching him from beside her bicycle.

For a few minutes, it seemed Betsy was wooed by his soft words as Leah had been. She'd never seen him as a deceiver. He'd never seemed that way. Apparently, Josiah had just been better at hiding his intent.

Her mouth pulling into a frown, she only wished she could stop pining for him.

He took several careful steps toward the mare and, just as it seemed she would stand still for his advances, the horse startled suddenly and jogged away.

53

Fueled by her body's unwelcomed response to him, Leah broke out in another peal of laughter.

Turning in her direction, Josiah braced his hands on his hips, saying with annoyance in his voice, "If you think you can do better, why don't you come get her?"

"You seem to be doing so well yourself," she sassed back, grinning.

Josiah took steady steps toward the edge of the pen, looking at Leah where she stood. He'd always been struck by her blue-eyed beauty, even though *Gott* bade them to consider more a person's soul. He wasn't the only *Mann* in Windber to take notice of her when she'd visited. At the time, he'd been amazed she'd chosen him.

The thought stabbed him in the chest.

Frustrated as well by his struggle to get the darned horse to behave, he took a deep breath, followed by another. Working in the heat of the 'smithy, he'd removed his jacket, chasing the horse in his shirt sleeves, suspenders holding up his serviceable pants.

This wasn't his best moment, or his best look, and he'd have given a lot to have beautiful Leah not see him chasing a stubborn horse. She'd broken his heart and he wasn't sure how to move on. Having to deal with her now felt like adding salt to the wound.

His chest still heaving a little from his exertions, he said tersely when she didn't respond to his question, "I thought not."

Her voice stopped him in the act of turning back to the sorrel when he heard her say, "Well, it sure looks as if you could use some help."

"From you?" Unimpressed, he let himself scan her.

She put what looked like a quilt back in the bicycle basket. "Do you think I couldn't?"

"I didn't say that." He'd once offered Leah what he'd never offered another woman, been with her in tender moments that shook him to remember. Then, she'd cruelly refused to understand his concerns and run off as if he'd been nothing to her. Thinking now of all they'd been to one another, he tasted ashes in his mouth.

Josiah drew another breath, still staring over the fence rail at her. It seemed important to stand his ground and not falter beneath her mocking scorn.

"Come on, then. Get in here and help with the stubborn thing. Maybe you can talk some sense into her—one stubborn *Maedel* to another."

"Very funny," she said, coming over to lift the latch on the gate. "Betsy just knows what's due her and she won't take less."

"What's due her? She needs new horseshoes. She's not a foal. She should be used to this."

With what sounded like a snort, Leah responded, "The horse doesn't know you. As far as she's concerned, you may mean her harm. Betsy's too smart to trust a stranger."

"I think you're giving the sorrel too much credit," he said in a dry tone, nodding toward the horse. "Go ahead, if you think you can do better. She knows you, I presume?"

"She does. She should, anyway." Leah circled the horse who sidled away from her, as well.

It might have been petty of him, but Josiah watched with silent pleasure as the horse proceeded to shy away from Leah, too.

"You've got her all riled up," Leah criticized.

"I can see she's very upset." He sardonically watched the sorrel skitter across the pen when Leah approached.

Several times, Leah moved toward her, using various approaches. Once, she even got a feed bag that hung outside the pen, trying to entice the horse.

"Here, sweet Betsy," she cooed. "Come here and try some yummy grain."

Betsy remained on the opposite side of the pen, her liquid brown eyes watchful.

At one point, Gideon came to the 'smithy door, lifting a hand to greet Leah. As she was in the middle of the pen, trying to coax the sorrel, she only waved back.

When she made her fifth or sixth unsuccessful attempt to snag the mare, Josiah stood to the side, a smile creasing his face. He felt vindicated by all this. Leah wasn't laughing at him now.

"Instead of just standing there like a *Debiel*," she snapped, "you could try to help me shoo her inside. We should be able to do it, if we work together."

"What exactly do you have in mind that hasn't been tried already?"

Several blonde tendrils had escaped her black *Kapp* and she looked a little frazzled.

"If I sent her running toward the 'smithy door, you can stand to one side and direct her, so when she turns to avoid you, she has nowhere to go, but inside."

"I can do that," he responded in a level tone after a few moments' consideration of her plan.

"*Gut*. You stand over there a few feet from the 'smithy door and drive her toward it."

"Okay. Send her my way and we'll see if we can get her inside."

"*Yah*," Leah walked away from the door, "I will stand in the back of the pen and wave my arms."

At this point, Josiah just wanted to get the horse where she belonged. He shifted to stand several feet to the side of the wide 'smithy door.

Standing near the fence on the far side of the pen, her big liquid eyes watchful, Betsy considered them.

"Okay," Leah called from the far side, "I'm going to run toward her alongside the edge of the pen. That should send her toward you and you can direct her inside."

Over to the side, Gideon stood in the 'smithy door, grinning as if he'd comprehended well the challenge they faced.

Not sure her plan would work, Josiah figured there was no harm in trying it. "Hopefully, this does the job."

He held his spot, startled by Leah running suddenly toward the horse, a ferocious expression on her easy-to-read face.

In the matter of seconds, they were in the middle of a noisy chaos with stamping hooves in flurry of movement.

"Yeehaw, you *Dumm hund*!"

Before he had time to decide if horses were insulted at being called dogs, he quickly took a step away from the big 'smithy door, hoping the horse didn't feel threatened by him and veer back toward Leah.

"You catch the mare when we get her inside!" Josiah yelled at Gideon, turning back to the pen.

"*Yah*." Gideon put down a rag, bracing for action.

56

"Gee! Gee! Gee!" Leah shrieked, staying close to the fence as she headed toward the building that held Gideon's forge.

With Leah running toward the horse like a demented thing, Betsy reared back her head several times in fear and dismay before she bolted away. With the fenced side of the pen keeping her from veering to the left, she had no choice but to turn toward Josiah.

As they'd hoped, the horse ran to his side of the pen, swinging toward the 'smithy when Josiah took a step forward, waving his arms. By this time, Leah yelled as she darted across the pen.

When a startled Betsy came running his way, Josiah flapped his arms to head her into the 'smithy door and Gideon was there to grab the mare.

Turning back to the pen, Josiah was startled to receive a stumbling Leah into his arms with a thump. Gasping from the impact, he fell back a foot or two, Leah's fragrant weight in his embrace.

A flood of memory shot through him, leaving Josiah breathless of a different sort altogether. She felt...so good in his arms.

It felt they were frozen together, caught for the beat of several long seconds. He could feel the thunder of her heartbeat, smell the sweet scent of her skin.

"Oh!" she exclaimed, hurriedly wedging her arms between them. "I'm so sorry! I was running fast and tripped."

His mind told him to release the arms he'd locked around her when she fell against him. Josiah obeyed slowly, knowing this was the prudent thing to do. The right thing...even though holding Leah like this felt more right to him that he'd felt in over a year.

Good grief, if nothing else, he needed to remember that Gideon was only a few feet away, tying Betsy to the horse post beside the forge.

"Of course." Josiah saw her stumble back out of his embrace, both regretful and relieved. "I should get inside to help your *Onkle* with the sorrel."

Just then, Gideon appeared in the wide 'smithy door. "Are...the two of you alright?"

His brows lifted, the ever-present grin on his face widened.

"*Yah.*" Josiah dropped his arms to his side, knowing his expression had gone wooden.

Gideon still grinned. "*Gut. Denki* to you both for convincing Betsy to come in."

Leah retied her apron, her cheeks red. She could have been blushing or her pinkness could be a result of running so hard.

Looking back and forth between the two of them, Leah's *Onkle* said before he turned to go back into the 'smithy, "I'm sure Betsy felt you both wanted to be alone."

*

Had she been wrong to keep Eli and Josiah apart?

The question leaping into her thoughts, Leah kept her gaze on the bishop at the meeting several days later. She hoped fervently that the heat in her cheeks after glancing Josiah's way would soon subside. Making a conscious choice not to do this again, she gripped Eli more closely until he wriggled in response.

Leah smiled down at her son, dropping a kiss on the sandy blond crown of his head as he clutched at a little faceless doll her *Bruder* had given him. Had she been wrong to keep him to herself? Maybe she should have sacrificed herself…married Josiah when he made the obligatory offer she was sure would have come.

To her dismay, when she and her son had come into the *Gruder's Haus* for church today, the toddler had gravitated to Josiah like lead to a magnet. For some reason, Josiah had chosen this moment to give his rare broad smile to the child. Naturally, Eli had gone right to him.

It was as if the two knew they were meant to be together. She was still shaking.

The rooms were still sparsely filled, since they were early. Even though Josiah had sat across the room with some other young *Menner* in the church, the small *Buwe* had somehow walked straight to the *Mann* she wanted most to ignore, reaching chubby hands to be lifted up.

She'd done her best to keep from Josiah that he had a son, even reminding herself that, if he should realize the significance of

Eli's age, she could lie and tell him she'd lain with an *Englischer* soon after being with him.

Just the thought of uttering this big lie left ashes on her tongue. *Gott* wanted his children to be truthful, but even in this?

Leah knew it was no good to avoid Gideon's shop all the time Josiah was here. She normally dropped in to see her *Onkle* several times a week. Changing that now—in an effort to avoid the kind of situation they'd had last time—would only make her look suspicious. She couldn't help realizing there was already talk of who had fathered Eli. *Yah*, they were also told to refrain from talking about one another, but it was only human that her situation garnered comment.

She'd had to cross the Gruder's family room to retrieve her son from the *Mann* who was his father. All the while feeling her cheeks redden as she walked over to get Eli, Leah had sent up prayers to be sustained and guided.

Had she been wrong to keep Eli and Josiah apart? The question just would not be dismissed, no matter how she tried.

He'd smiled down at her son with such kindness, yet this was the *Mann* who'd angrily insisted on not telling his *Mamm* he was to marry Leah.

Time, Josiah insisted, would help his mother get used to the idea. Get used to the idea of him doing as *Gott* directed?

Leah drew in a deep breath, trying to calm herself, lifting her chin to give rapt attention to the speaker. She knew her face was too readable.

She'd always thought Josiah would be a loving and generous *Daed*, but then he'd used her for his own pleasure and chosen his *Mamm's* comfort over Leah's.

Yah, they were to be respectful of one another and offer kindness, but his actions had seemed wrong to her. Still seemed wrong, but wondering about her own actions was unavoidable. All were weak, at times. Was she examining the speck in her neighbor's eye, while ignoring the board in her own?

Maybe, she could have made the wrong choice not to tell Josiah she was with child. She'd certainly been wrong to run away from her life.

In her distressed mind, she'd felt then that Eli was better off without her...so, she'd run away to the *Englischer* world.

Now, it seemed she faced Josiah at every turn and, *Gott* help her, she dreamed of him at night in her narrow bed. Ached for the *Mann* she thought she'd found in him.

Chapter Six

Ada
Windber

The August sun intermittently shining warm on her *Kapp* as they drove, Ada settled more securely into the seat next to Luke. The buggy jostled along down the drive from the *Haus* that ran under the shade of tall white pines intermingled with the sturdier oaks.

Wedged between the two of them sat five-year-old, Mary Grace Stoll, Luke's granddaughter by his youngest *Dochder*. Since the child and her *Eldre* lived in Ohio, Ada had been surprised to see her in Luke's buggy that morning.

A little thrown off balance at the girl's unexpected presence, Ada sent her a tight smile. It was silly to feel this way with a child, but she'd never been good at making conversation with strangers. Even small ones.

She braced her feet around the stoppered ceramic crock of sweet pickles on the buggy floorboard, clenching it between the folds of her gray skirt around her knees. Hopefully, her barrel of hot pickles was secure in the back of the buggy.

Glancing at the *Mann* driving the buggy, his tanned face shaded by the wide brim of his hat, she said primly, "Thank you for taking the time to drive me to Pickle Fest. I know you have work to do on the farm...and apparently have an out-of-town guest, too. I didn't know."

Giving Mary Grace a wink, Luke grinned at Ada. "Are you kidding? Of course, we are driving you. This is a nice break for me and my *Kinskind*. A sunny summer day. A visit to Pickle Fest. How could we turn this down? *Yah*, Mary Grace? I'm sure you had no idea of the fun you'd have when you came to visit your old *Grossdaddi*."

Mary Grace smiled at him, her face sunny and penny-bright beneath her small, black *Kapp*. "You are always so fun, *Grossdaddi*. I can hardly wait to see the Pickle Fest!"

Smiling at her and then at Ada, Luke confided, "Mary Grace's *Mamm* just had matched twins and my *Dochder* thought

61

Mary Grace—being too young to help much—might be better visiting here for a few days."

"Of course." Ada felt less ruffled then, at this addition to their trip. Unexpected changes always startled her, but this child was as fun and lively as her *Grossdaddi*. Josiah had been such a solemn child—not unexpected given the circumstances in his youth. Being with a very different *Kinder* left her feeling off kilter now, but not unpleasantly so.

Cooler air brushed her cheek when they again entered the shade of tall pines.

Smoothing her brown skirt with one hand, Ada glanced at the smiling little girl. She said to the child, "The Pickle Fest games and activities can be fun and we all know here that your *Grossdaddi* can be very silly."

The girl giggled.

"*Yah*," Luke said. "There are games and competitions. Even a pickle eating contest."

Wrinkling her nose, Mary Grace commented, "I guess that could be fun, although I don't think I'd like to eat a lot of pickles."

"It is fun to watch! *Frau* Miller has won the Best Hot Pickle Contest four times," Luke confided to the girl. "I myself prefer sweet pickles."

"And thereby I won $50 each year," Ada said, "which is the important thing."

Even her stern older sister, Judith, had applauded her pickles.

"*Yah*," Luke concurred, sliding a glance her way "Ada's pickles are truly the best. Very tasty. Particularly the sweet ones."

He grinned at Ada.

Mary Grace giggled at his laughing tone.

"Keep your eyes on the road," Ada recommended, rolling her eyes.

As usual, not fazed by her tart words, Luke just laughed.

With the hollow sound of boards beneath the buggy horse's hooves, they crossed a picturesque covered bridge that spanned a dark river, tumbling into a small waterfall beyond the bridge. In late summer, the river surface lazily carried several faded leaves drifting by on its surface.

Soon they rounded a corner and trotted into the shady glen beside the road that held the sprawl of Pickle Fest booths.

Drawing in a breath of Pickle Fest air, Ada reflected on the general fun giddiness of it all. Happy voices rose all around them as they pulled into the parking area, others hurrying into the festival grounds. Off in the distance, music from some ride jangled. Even the parking lot air smelled of frying pickles mixed with the scent of sweet fried doughnuts. Brightly colored banners fluttered from wires running around the booth enclosure.

Rows of booths ran along an enclosure and the rides could be seen beyond these.

Along with several other buggies, Luke parked under the shade of branches that stretched tall limbs into the parking area from a nearby wooded acre.

"We need to get your pickles to the competition booth first," he said, "then we can look around."

"*Denki*," Ada said. "The pickle competition booth should be up front."

"I'll get the barrels there right away." Luke sent her a reassuring smile that seemed to Ada almost caressing. She shook her thoughts loose from the impression with the reminder thought that Luke was an old friend. Just a very old friend.

He helped his *Kinskind* to the ground and then wrestled the barrels out of the rear of the buggy, easily tucking one under each of his arms. Not for the first time, Ada noted that Luke was a well-built *Mann*, a true testament of *Gott's* skill.

"Would you hold Mary Grace by the hand? Since both mine are busy, at the moment." He smiled at Ada.

"Of course." Reaching out, Ada took the girl's small hand, thinking it had been a long while since she'd done this with a *Kinder*. Mary Grace's hand felt so small in hers.

"First, we do this, Mary Grace," Luke confided to his grandchild. "Then, we'll all take a walk to look around. *Yah*, Ada?"

"Yes." Aware of feeling unusually buoyant, she smiled down at Mary Grace.

She always enjoyed Luke's company, although this usually involved him working around the farm.

After they'd left her pickle barrel for the competition, the three strolled along the booths.

Pickle Fest visitors clogged the walkway in front of them, shifting as they passed, some stopping to look at the wares displayed in the booths.

Ada's sister, Judith, stood down the row in close conversation with a woman in Amish garb that Ada recognized as from a distant farm.

Waving at her *Schweschder*, she got a nod in return as Judith turned back to her friend.

"Look there," Luke told his *Kinskind*, "there's a pancake breakfast being offered."

The girl gave him a cheerful smile. "You gave me breakfast. Remember? I'm not very hungry now."

Luke laughed. "I suppose not, although I'd think pancakes would be hard to turn down."

Another competition booth appeared in the row before them, advertising a contest to determine the best Amish buttermilk cookie in the county.

"Ada!" He looked over. "Did you not enter this? Your buttermilk cookies are the best I've ever tasted. You'd be sure to win."

Squelching the pleasure that shot up in her at Luke's claim, she shook her head. "There's no cash prize for the cookie contest...and no reason, other than pride, to enter."

"Maybe not," he conceded, "but it seems a shame not to share *Gott's* gift of your cookie making skills."

Feeling herself blush like a *Youngie*, she aimed for a stringent response. "Don't try to flatter me, Luke Fisher. You know that cookie recipe was my *Mamm's*. Why any of my *Schweschders* could make them as well."

"Their cookies probably don't taste as wonderful," he claimed with a wicked smile. "Your love of baking them has to seep into the cookies and make them extra-special tasty. Why you're famous for them."

"Don't be ridiculous," she responded.

He walked along beside her, the little girl between them gawking at the sights.

"You're telling me you don't enjoy making the cookies?" Luke laughed. "You forget, I've seen you—covered in flour and joyfully baking them."

She didn't know what to say, the image flashing through her mind of the last time she'd baked cookies, her *Kapp* askew and her apron spotted with cookie debris. Luke had come by to find Josiah for some farm business.

"There was *budder* on your cheek," he said, as if the same memory echoed in his mind.

Flushing, her body suddenly feeling warm, Ada suddenly pointed to a roped-off area, "I saw they've set up a treasure hunt for children. Over here. See?"

"Oh, yes!" Mary Grace clutched at her grandfather's hand. "Can we do that?"

He smiled down at the child indulgently. "Of course, *Liebling*. The booth opens in an hour or two."

Looking around, they walked along the first row of booths and Ada spied Miriam Yoder, setting up a booth with quilts of all colors. Ada and Miriam often quilted together with several other Amish women, including Judith when she could get free of her chores.

The back of the sturdy, buxom woman was visible as she stretched to hang a quilt over the edge of the booth.

"*Goedemorgen*, Miriam," Ada called out as they neared the booth hung with sturdy white and cream quilts, along with some made with navy and dark brown pieces.

Her friend turned quickly, a quilt of medium and sky blue in her arms. "Ada! And Luke Fisher! What a nice surprise to see you here."

"You have a good display," Luke commented. "I can see you've been busy."

"*Yah*, and Ada has been a big part of it," the pink-cheeked, blue-eyed woman said, beaming at them. "See, Ada? I put the large checked one we just finished right up front."

"I see that. It looks *gut* and warm." Ada smiled back at her friend, trying not to feel self-conscious about being there with Luke. "I hope it brings good value."

Miriam nodded enthusiastically, "*Yah*! So do I."

"Are you running the booth alone?"

65

Almost before the words left Ada's mouth her sister, Judith, rounded the corner of the quilt booth.

Ada greeted her. "Judith!"

"*Yah. Goedemorgen*," the other woman responded, following her acknowledgment by saying in an austere tone, "I said I'd help Miriam here today."

As she too often did with Judith, Ada felt chastened. "Yes, you did."

"And who is this little *Maedel*?" Miriam smiled at the girl clutching Luke's pant leg.

Luke's hand rested on Mary Grace's shoulder. "This is my *Dochder's* girl, Mary Grace. You know my Abigail just had twins?"

"*Neh*! What a blessing from *Gott*!" Miriam exclaimed.

"That particular blessing comes with much work," Judith said.

"It is a blessing," Luke nodded, "but you are right. Having two little *Bopplin* at the same time does make for a lot of work. Abigail sent Mary Grace to visit me while she and her husband get things sorted out."

Miriam reached down, beaming still as she shook the small girl's hand. "So, you came with your *Grossdaddi* to the Pickle Fest?"

Mary Grace nodded, smiling brightly as she did so.

Ada noted that even her stern sister's face softened when she looked at the girl.

"This is *gut*!" Miriam put a hand to her ample waist. "Are you planning to enter the goat milking contest? My girls would have loved it when they were younger!"

Judith nodded, a wry smile on her lips. "Mine, too."

"Goat milking contest?" Luke echoed.

Miriam nodded vigorously. "*Yah*. And the winner gets a cash prize."

"How much?" Ada asked, the question popping out of her.

"Ah, only twenty-five dollars, I think." Miriam made a face, "but that's something."

"It is," Ada agreed, glancing at Luke. "I think Abigail would be glad of a little extra, right now."

"I would think so." Judith considered the situation.

66

Jumping up and down as she held her *Grossdaddi's* hand, Mary Grace squealed. "A goat! I can milk a goat. If I win, *Grossdaddi*, I could give *Daed* and *Mamm* some help!"

"You could, indeed, child." He smiled down at her.

"But...I've never milked a goat myself." Her smile faded a little. "*Mamm* was just starting to teach me to milk when the twins came early," she confided to Ada. "We have several cows and it's going to be my job to care for them."

The girl paused a moment, her sunny face fading a little more. "They are very big, though. Goats aren't that big."

Judith agreed, "Cows are bigger than goats."

Mary Grace tugged again on Luke's hand to ask anxiously. "Do you think the contest people will let you help me?"

He made a musing expression. "They might since you are such a small *kinder*. We can ask."

"Oh, good. *Mamm* and *Daed* will be so glad."

Watching Luke and the girl, Ada couldn't help remembering Josiah at this age. A more serious child, he'd grown up into a strong, handsome *Mann*.

If only he could find the right Maedel... The thought streaked past.

"The milking contest registration is just over there." Miriam stretched out her arm to indicate a booth several down the way.

They went to sign her up as Mary Grace chattered a little nervously. Miriam had directed them to the spot accurately and several pairs of girls waited to sign the sheet.

As they stood in line behind the others, Luke fell silent. This was so unlike him that Ada glanced over curiously. The man spun silly banter most the day, particularly with this child, she'd noticed.

Not sure what Luke's silence indicated, Ada said, "This should be fun. You and Mary Grace working together to milk a small creature."

As the child swung in blithe ignorance on his hand, Luke looked over at Ada. "*Yah*. Sure."

Something in his voice made her say, "But...?"

67

Leaning toward her and lowering his voice, as if trying to keep his words from the child, he said, "But these are all *Maedels*, Ada. I'm not a *Maedel*."

"*Neh*." A thread of humor ran through the word. Clear as day, he was not a young girl.

Luke said into her ear. "Do you think this will be fair? I've been milking—both goats and cows—longer than these children have been alive. Probably longer than their *Eldre* have been alive."

"You're being silly," she told him.

Ada glanced at the teams of pairs of giggling, chattering girls in line in front of them. He had a point.

She looked down then at the small *Kinder* swinging on his arm. In an equally quiet tone, she said. "I see what you mean, but you can't disappoint Mary Grace."

His face worried, Luke held her gaze. "*Neh*. *Neh*, but this doesn't feel right. These girls have feelings, too."

Not responding as they shuffled forward with the movement of the line, Ada considered his dilemma. He was a sympathetic, kind *Mann*. She could understand the predicament.

Still not sure what to say, she stood in line behind him, his little granddaughter oblivious to his discomfort.

Here Luke was, a fully grown, adult man. Of course, a milking competition between someone who'd milked for thirty-years or more and girls who'd been doing this for five years wouldn't be fair.

"Oh, *Grossdaddi*," Mary Grace gushed, "this looks like so much fun! I get to milk goats with older girls!"

Ada saw him swallow. The "older girls" the child referred to were maybe eight or ten-year-olds.

The *Mann* was stuck between a rock and a hard place and Ada saw that embarrassment reddened his cheeks.

"Maybe I could do it," she blurted out. "Be in the contest with Mary Grace."

He whipped around to look at her.

"I'm not a young girl," she said with gruffly, "but at least I'm a girl. Maybe I won't stand out as much."

"You'd do this?" Luke asked Ada.

"*Yah*, of course," she responded as easily as she could.

Luke stared at Ada, relief flooding over his features.

68

Feeling a flush of warmth run over her cheekbones, as he looked at her in growing excitement, she briefly wondered why she'd made the offer. Mary Grace was so young, entering the contest had to be futile and awkward. Two things Ada generally avoided, not wanting to seem silly.

In this case, that didn't seem to matter.

Luke stood next to her, a thankful smile spreading across his face. "*Yah*! That would work well! You two could be a team."

Ada nodded, berating herself for getting goofy over a *Mann* who'd probably never thought of her romantically.

"That we can be. Better me than you. Come, Mary Grace." She offered the child her hand, the corner of her mouth lifting at the familiar feel of small fingers curling around hers. Together, they made their way toward the sign-up table.

"Look at the cute little goats!" Mary Grace exclaimed, bouncing in her excitement.

"They're still bigger than you, *Leibling*. Are you sure you won't be frightened to milk one? Sometimes they kick."

"Oh, *Grossdaddi*, they are animals. They probably just don't understand." The small girl said wisely, "My *Mamm* said the cows get uncomfortable if they're not milked. Goats are like that, too, aren't they?"

Sending Ada a warm, grateful look, Luke knelt before the girl.

Ada crouched beside Mary Grace. "Your *Mamm* is right, honey. Cows and goats need milking or they hurt, but your *Grossdaddi* is right, too. Goats do kick sometimes."

"I don't care," the girl said stoutly. "I'd like to try."

"What if," Luke said, squatting down next to her, "what if Ada—*Frau* Miller—helped you in the contest instead of me? It looks like this is a girl-thing."

Mary Grace looked doubtful for a moment, glancing at Ada and then to the line of girls signing up for the contest. "All these girls will also milk goats?"

"*Yah*," Ada said, glancing up at what looked to Luke like six or seven girls, several standing to the side of the older, worn-looking woman who was in charge of signing up contestants. Off to the right, an open-air metal pavilion held half a dozen or maybe

69

eight goat milking stands and goats could be heard bleating in the background.

For a considering moment, Mary Grace stared at them before turning back to Ada. "The others are all older than me. Do you know you know how to milk goats good? As good as *Grossdaddi*?"

Smiling at this question, Ada assured her. "I do. I've milked many in my day. Never been bested by a goat, I promise."

"And you can keep them from kicking us?" Mary Grace asked gravely.

"I can...and keep them from kicking over the milk can." If she'd been applying for a job, Ada couldn't have had a more serious expression.

"Okay," the small girl agreed, "as long as you watch, *Grossdaddi*."

"Wild horses couldn't drag me away," he promised without hesitation. "I'll stand right over there."

"If we're going to sign up," Ada said, again holding her hand out to Mary Grace, "we should do it now as the contest starts soon. Let's get into the line."

"Let's do it! I'll bet with you helping me, we can win the prize."

Ada laughed. "I hope we can."

"I'll be right here, as you asked," Luke called out as the two moved forward in the sign-up line.

In no time, Ada and Mary Grace stood in front of the small sign-up table. She saw out of the corner of her eye that Luke pulled at his beard, nervously, as Ada took the girl's hand, speaking to the woman behind the table. The woman nodded after a moment, understanding her request to participate with the child. Then Luke's *Kinskind*, still holding Ada's hand, moved to the group of others in the contest.

There was Pickle Fest merriment around them, the hustle and bustle boisterous on the path outside the goat corral, even though the contestants seemed to know to be quiet near the animals.

When it was time to start the competition, all the girls went into the pavilion, some *Englischers* in jeans and several Amish

Maedels with their aprons over long, muted skirts and black *Kapps* on their heads.

Ada positioned the girl beside her. She talked to Mary Grace about the importance of cleaning the goat's udder before milking, intent as she directed the girl.

"See? We use these to clean her. First, the wet rag and then dry her udder with one from the dry pile." She gestured to the bucket that held damp rags for wiping the goat.

Several older girls moved their goats around with practiced aplomb, seeming old hands at this. As other girls shifted on their milking stools and readied themselves, an *Englischer* man unhooked a gate and began to lead goats to the stands. Soon, a brown-spotted goat was led to Mary Grace's stand.

As Luke watched a little anxiously from the fence that lined the corral, Ada dumped a portion of the feed provided into the feeding bucket attached to their stand. Having done this a hundred times, Ada moved the head piece to secure the goat in the stand.

All the contestants attended to their animals, giving them food to keep them content and washing them before starting to milk.

Going to the rear of the animal, Ada hooked several provided ropes around the brown-spotted goat's hind legs. No matter how she tried, the little goat couldn't move her hooves much. Mary Grace's eyes grew wide with comprehension, looking relieved that she wouldn't have to worry about their goat kicking her.

Remembering from the sign next to the entry table, the contest would be judged by both speed and the amount of milk drained from the goats, Ada calmly moved to sit on the stool. She wasn't sure how they knew these goats all gave the same amount of milk, but it didn't matter, as winning this contest wasn't her biggest concern.

"Come, Mary Grace." She smiled at the child. "Stand close to me, right here at my shoulder, and I'll show you how to milk this girl."

She ran a calming hand over the goat's flank.

"*Denki, Frau* Miller."

"We take hold of the goat's teat like this. See? Hold her firmly. She doesn't mind, at all. You try it."

The child leaned forward, such a serious, intent look on her face that Ada had to suppress a smile.

"Like this?"

"*Yah.* Maybe shift your hand up a little higher. Now squeeze gently and pull down on the teat. Yes! Like that. Maybe you can do one side and I'll do the other?"

"Okay."

"After you milk a while, and the stream seems to get a little weaker," she said, moving around to the back of the brown goat, "we're going to jostle her udder."

Mary Grace's face was watchful and serious.

"I'll look like I'm being rough, but this won't hurt her. She wants us to drain it all."

The child nodded, still round-eyed and serious.

Moving back to sit on the short milking stool, Ada shifted the silver bowl provided for the goat milk. "I'll do the first teat and then you do the second. Stay right here beside me."

"I will," Mary Grace promised.

"Ladies!" The woman who'd registered the contest entrants stepped up to a table at the front of the open-air building, speaking into a microphone and announcing, "We are about to start. You'll have fifteen minutes before time to stop is called. If you finish more quickly, points will be added to your score, but only if the goat is fully-milked. Are you ready? Okay, start!"

Ada reached forward, Mary Grace beside her, to quickly dip into the bowl of wet rags and start washing the goat's udder and teats. She handed the girl a rag after a moment and Mary Grace leaned in to rub it on the goat's underside.

The others in the contest were now milking their goats, but Ada focused on including her small shadow in the action. After the washing, she began milking their brown-spotted goat.

"See how this works, Mary Grace? We just keep tugging."

"She-she doesn't seem to mind it." The girl's gaze was on the goat.

"*Neh,*" Ada smiled at the child, "this helps her feel much better. Here. You give it a try."

She reached out to place Mary Grace between her knees. "Put your hands here and, yes, here. Now pull the way I showed you. *Yah*, that's right. Just tug a little harder."

Around them, milk could be heard filling the other contestants' bowls, solid squirts making metallic sounds. Ada ignored this and the calls from their audience. It had been years since she'd taught such a basic chore to a child. Mary Grace was intent, the downy curve of her cheek right at Ada's eye level as she looked over the girl's shoulder.

She felt a swelling warmth in her chest and flashed a glance over at Luke, standing as close as he could in the fenced-off audience. He smiled warmly, his gaze brimming with gratitude and something else that made Ada feel heat crawl into her cheeks again.

Turning back to the goat, she tried to focus on the job at hand. Mary Grace steadily pulled at the teats with her small hands. The goat must have been an easy milker, because a stream of milk streamed into the bowl with every tug. They'd never win at this pace. Ada could have raced ahead of the other girls, given that she'd been milking longer than they'd been alive. Instead, she kept Luke's little *Kinskind* in the game.

When each tug began to yield smaller streams, she told the girl, "Hold on a moment, Mary Grace."

Ada moved to the back of the goat's roped feet, jostling the goat's udder to release what was left of its milk. Seeing an anxious look descend onto the child's face, she assured her, "This doesn't hurt the goat, you know. She'll feel all better if we get every drip out of her."

"Oh!" Mary Grace said, "It looked like you were hitting her back there."

"*Neh*," Ada responded, stepping back to the brown goat's side to give her udder a few more tugs, "I wouldn't do that. Goats need their udders jiggled to get all the milk out."

She moved back, sitting down on the stool to encourage Mary Grace to squeeze the rest of the milk out of the goat's teats.

In a few minutes, the participants were signaled to stop.

After the woman at the microphone called time, several helpers gathered the bowls of milk to take to the front table for measuring. From the crestfallen faces, it was clear that several hadn't finished with their goats.

Glancing around, Ada saw that most of the other *Maedels* had finished, however, and now sat back on their stools. She knew some goats gave more milk naturally, but she hoped the goats used were chosen to have a similar production.

Several people behind the table solemnly measured each bowl, an array of measuring cups in front of them.

In a few minutes, the same careworn woman stepped back to the microphone with a clipboard in her hand. "All the bowls handed in have been measured and…we have a winner."

Ada squeezed Luke's *Kinskind's* shoulder, seeing that the child looked a little worried. "You did a gut job, Mary Grace."

"Our winner," the woman at the microphone said impressively is…Kayla Woodsmore from Meadville!"

Those standing in the perimeter around the corral clapped and hooted as an Englischer girl stepped forward to accept the prize.

"We also have a special prize," the microphone woman said, stepping back after giving the winner her envelope. "We'd like to award our youngest contestant, Mary Grace Lehman and her helper, Ada Miller!"

Flushing with a pride that surprised her, Ada watched Mary Grace's little form walk seriously up to the woman at the microphone.

"Thank you, Mary Grace," the woman said. "We hope you'll continue to enter our yearly contest."

Luke felt transfixed, watching Ada with Mary Grace. His heart swelled as he stood at the sidelines, seeing her smile as his small granddaughter received her special prize. He wished anyone who'd ever thought Ada was chilly could see her at this moment.

He released a breath it felt he'd been holding all through the contest. It wouldn't have been the end of the child's day if Mary Grace hadn't won anything, at all, but he was relieved, just the same.

Working on young Josiah's farm had held a different kind of complexity. Ada was grieving in the beginning and had kept watchful eyes on her son since then.

Experience over the years, of course, had taught him that Ada was much more than she seemed. Even though she could be tart, she was smart and had a kind heart. She just liked to keep this somewhat hidden. He supposed, given the heartache she'd been through, he could understand that. He couldn't imagine losing a child. Losing two wives had been hard enough.

He wanted to grab Ada up in a kiss, he'd been so glad at her suggestion that she could enter the contest with his *Kinskind*. Of course, the urge to kiss Ada had gripped him multiple times and he was, thus, prepared to resist it. She was undoubtedly a beautiful woman and, although *Gott* directed them to seek the inner beauty inside, a charming appearance couldn't completely be overlooked.

All through the contest, he'd had eyes only for the one taller entrant with a white *Kapp* on her head and Mary Grace by the hand. His heart swelled in his chest and he tried not to look as moved as he felt.

Luke knew Ada Miller. She wasn't a public woman and was modest, even more than others in the Amish faith, not putting herself forward in pride. Yet, she had volunteered to help his young granddaughter.

She had a golden heart, that woman. It just wasn't always easy to see.

*

Josiah
Mannheim

The late summer sun beat down on his bare head as Josiah took a few minutes outside the 'smithy after his lunch before going back inside. Gideon was a *gut* teacher, but Josiah didn't yet feel very handy at the work.

He balanced easily on the top rail of the fenced area near the 'smithy, his mind straying to Leah, as it too often did. Her wrangling that mare into the 'smithy with him had brought up all his old feelings. His and Leah's last moments as a promised couple replayed in his mind and he wondered again about the choices presented him.

She'd left him. He'd loved her and she'd left.

Josiah's jaw tightened and he could feel the muscle there throb, even as his heart felt bruised in his chest.

Leah deserved that he should turn his back on her, but he couldn't do that. Why couldn't he?

Why could he not forget her and move on? How could he have been so wrong about her? The question brought a resounding conviction inside him that he *hadn't* been wrong. But then, how could she not see she'd been unreasonable?

The sound of a twig snapping nearby brought up Josiah's head and, as if his thoughts had conjured her presence, he spied Leah coming out of the wooded area behind the 'smithy, her black *Kapp* neat on her head. As Gideon was her *Onkle*, he'd seen her at the 'smithy several times.

This was no different. He felt as if time spun down to a stop and he could hear the slow thump, thump of his sore heart.

She seemed suddenly to sense she wasn't alone, stopping to raise her hand to shade her eyes.

"You!" Leah uttered in a scathing tone. Her jaw hardening, she came forward. "I've come to see my *Onkle*."

Stupidly, all he could think to say was, "Oh."

His heart still thumping heavily at seeing her, Josiah watched her stalk past him. Her clean, wholesome scent wafted to him in the air and he found himself asking, "Why do you hate me so much, Leah?"

"What did you say?" She turned to stare.

Every word that came out of her when she spoke to him seemed coated with anger.

Josiah took a deep breath, repeating his question. "Why do you hate me so much?"

She looked at him for a moment, her lips thinning. "Well, Josiah, it could have to do with you choosing your *Mamm* over me last year."

"I did not," he retorted. "That's ridiculous. I never said that. In front of *Gott*, I never did that!"

Leah braced her hand on her hip. "Yes, you did!"

"What I said was," he responded with carefully chosen words, "that we'd announce our plan to marry to my *Mamm* after she got to know you better."

"I spent four weeks in Windber back then. I met most of your friends and relatives many times. Your *Mamm* never had any interest in getting to know me then. Why would you think that would change?"

"It would have," he said stubbornly. "My *Mamm* doesn't warm up to anyone quickly. She's just that way. She needs to be comfortable."

Leah took a step toward him, reproach burning in her eyes. "That's just it, Josiah. *She needs!* Did you ever stop to think—or care about—what I needed? You asked me to be your wife, to share your life and be the mother to your children. Yet by asking me to wait, to keep from all our decision to wed, you were clear about who would always be first with you. You even came here with her—like a sweet little lamb—to find a wife your *Mamm* decided on for you."

Her voice held a scathing note and she looked at him as if he were a slimy slug on the ground.

"That is not true!" Josiah shot back.

"And you used a matchmaker to find this wife?" She smirked.

When he scrambled to find a response to this, Leah went on, "If Hagar had met your *Mamm's* requirements, you'd have asked her to be your wife."

"No," he said, his voice strong.

She advanced a step closer, pointing her finger at him. "You are not a *Mann*, Josiah. I didn't realize it then, but you do what she tells you, like a *Kinder*."

"I am not a child," Josiah rejected the accusation angrily. "*Yah*, I came here with my *Mamm*, but I had no interest or plans to ask Hagar to marry me."

"That's probably why you're here now." Leah went on as if he hadn't spoken, the words spilling out of her, hot and fast. "Maybe your *Mamm* sent you to steal her from my *Onkle*. Is Hagar more attractive now that Gideon is to marry her?"

"No. *Neh*, I'm not here because of her. I came here so Gideon could teach me blacksmithing," he said, his voice firm.

77

Josiah kept to himself the reality that he'd needed to leave his farm and his town for his *Mamm* to get the message that he didn't need her to choose a wife for him.

His mouth snapped shut. He couldn't tell Leah this.

Was she right? Had he been wrong to expect Leah to wait?

For several long minutes, they stood in the buggy drive outside the 'smithy—neither speaking, their gazes locked. An early autumn breeze shifted past, carrying a hint of cooler weather.

Josiah stared at her, Leah's black *Kapp* framing her heated face.

"So, you do hate me."

"*Yah*," she confirmed intensely before blurting, "but it isn't just…that."

The final word seemed to trickle out of her, trailing off to silence.

He frowned. "What else, then?"

Quietness fell between them again and her words that finally erupted seemed torn out of her. Her face reflected a bitter turmoil. "Because…because I made a terrible choice with you, Josiah. A terrible, life-altering choice."

Her anguished tone startled him, the sun hot on his shoulders through his white shirt. He didn't know how to respond. She sounded…hurt and upset more than angry…and, stupidly, he immediately wanted to comfort her. In a flash of a second, his brain reminded him of the sweetness of her kisses, the tender feel of her pressed against him that one afternoon.

How he'd missed her.

"I foolishly," she said finally, "thought you and I would become man and wife."

Her bitter smile twisted with these words.

Josiah felt the wave of her pain and remorse as if it were a physical thing hitting him and he still didn't know what to say, either to her earlier anger or the luminous picture her words conjured—the two of them married and in love.

"For the record," he managed to say, "I never changed my mind, Leah. You were the one who left."

A sad smile crossed her face.

"With you, I sinned. We sinned," she said as if he hadn't spoken. She seemed unaware that her words turned a knife in his gut.

Josiah's jaw firmed. "I asked you to marry me."

She went on, still not responding to his words. "I fornicated with you and broke my covenant with *Gott* and I cannot forgive myself for this."

"Leah. I never changed my mind. I also saw a future of us sharing a life together."

"*Yah*," she said. "*Eventually*. You, your mother and me. It is not a life I could tolerate. Not a partnership as *Gott* intended, I believe."

"Are we not to honor our parents?" Josiah retorted.

"To honor our *Eldre* is to live an honorable, righteous life. To be *gut* people," she shot back. "We are not to do exactly what our parents direct. Are they not human—and imperfect? We are told to strive to hear *Gott's* voice more than that of our *Eldre*!"

Not exactly sure how to respond, he said, "But we are not to disregard those who raised us."

"It's of no use to talk about it. I sinned and am now broken, thanks to you," she said simply. "How can you say otherwise? My sin was great. I lay with you, even though we aren't married. We didn't marry, after all."

Her words still hovering in the warm air between them, she threw a mournful, scorching look at him before turning back to the 'smithy door.

"Wait," he called out, hating the self-recrimination in her voice. Hating that this ugliness inside her was associated with him.

She'd made demands. *Were they so unreasonable?* The question whispered through his brain.

When she turned to look at him, he blurted out, "Leah, we are all broken. Not just you. As human beings, we are all broken. Me, too. I sinned along with you."

Again, silence beat between them, he said, "You are not more of a sinner than the rest."

He knew she couldn't argue with his claim. *Gott* recommended all to be chaste until marriage. It had been the two of them who had broken that covenant, although it hadn't seemed that way, at the time. They were simply two young people in love, planning to marry. Expressing that love in the most basic way had seemed right.

"*Yah*, more than the rest," she finally retorted. After a moment, she added, "It is I who bore the greatest punishment. Me."

*

Still wrestling with his conversation with Leah, Josiah chose not to go into the 'smithy where he knew she was with Gideon. He didn't understand her last statement. Instead of returning to his work, he adjusted the broad-brimmed hat on his head and walked up the slight incline to the *Haus* Hagar shared with her *Mamm*. He knew that Hagar and Gideon were to marry in several months and, despite Leah's accusations, he had no interest in disrupting these plans. They seemed very right together. Hagar had become his *gut* friend. Nothing more.

With the vague notion of visiting with her until Leah left the blacksmith shed, he went in the kitchen door, feeling frustrated when he heard unknown voices from the nearby living room. Hagar and Esther had guests sitting there with the them, but escaping out the way he'd come it wasn't an option as the kitchen had a pass-through to the living area. He knew he was visible to the women with Hagar and her mother.

"Josiah!" Hagar beckoned to him as she spied him in the kitchen. "Come meet our guests, if you haven't already."

Carrying his broad-brimmed hat between his fingers, Josiah pushed open the swinging kitchen door into the living area where a family of a mother and several *Kinder* visited with Hagar and Esther. He nodded toward the elderly of the women. "*Goedemorgen*, Miss Esther. Hagar."

"*Goedemorgen*, Josiah." Beaming at him in her frank way, Hagar came forward amid the chorus of greetings from the others. "Have you met Kate Miller and her *Dochders*, Sarah and Elizabeth? You may have seen them at church meetings."

Although he'd gone to church with Gideon only two days before, Josiah hadn't met many there. His acute awareness of Leah's presence distracted him from looking around.

He smiled and nodded at the dark-haired woman, her white *Kapp* neat on her head, her belly protruding in the family way. "I believe I met your husband. Enoch, *yah?*"

"Yes." Kate Miller smiled.

"This little *Maedel*," Hagar pointed to a girl of three or four clinging close to her *Mamm's* skirt, "is Elizabeth."

"*Goedemorgen*, Elizabeth," Josiah said, smiling at the shy child with grave respect.

"And this," Hagar gestured toward a *Maedel* of twelve or thirteen, "is Sarah."

Having bent to brush a kiss on Esther's lined cheek, he turned, "*Goedemorgen* to you, as well, Sarah Miller."

The girl nodded with a smile as Josiah followed Hagar's invitation to seat himself.

"Gideon has given you a break from the heat of the forge?" Hagar asked.

"*Yah.*"

"Well, we're glad you walked over. Kate and the girls were at the quilting gathering *Mamm* and I went to this morning."

On the rug between Kate Miller and Esther sat a sturdy, solemn brown-haired child of twelve or thirteen months, dressed in a tiny set of pants and jacket those worn by all *Menner*.

"And this little *Boppli* is your son?" He glanced at Kate with a smile.

"*Neh.*" Hagar laughed. "Eli is Leah's son. She let me bring him home from our quilting session, since she had several errands to run. Gideon and I raised Eli for her while Leah was away."

"Leah's son?" The smile was wiped from Josiah's face. "Gideon's *Nibling*? That Leah?"

Since the same names were often given to children of different families, the question wasn't odd, although Josiah felt suddenly very odd, a buzzing in his ears.

Hagar nodded cheerfully. "*Yah*, that Leah."

"Oh," he must not have sounded as strange as he felt since the women weren't staring at him, "but she isn't married. She wears a black *Kapp*…"

A sudden silence fell over the small group and he was acutely aware that none of the women in the room looked directly at him.

81

Only Hagar acted normal. "Leah and Eli were quilting with us. Not little Eli, of course. We are blessed to have her—I learn sewing tricks from Leah all the time. She has such neat, tiny stitches."

Josiah fell silent, his head buzzing with questions as Esther began speaking of the canning she hoped to do soon.

"Did you see the large pumpkin Isaac and Mercy have growing in their patch?" Kate asked, her eyes opening as if to stare in surprise at the big gourd.

"I did hear tell of it," Hagar said, reaching to pick up the *Boppli* who crawled to her.

"*Onkle* Isaac says it must weigh fifty pounds, at least," the *Maedel* Sarah interpolated in an excited voice. "I know I've never seen one as large."

Josiah sat silent as his thoughts swirled. Leah had a child? And no husband?

After a few more minutes of visiting, Kate, Sarah and the shy *Boppli*, Elizabeth, prepared to leave.

"It was so nice to meet you, Josiah. I hope we see you again soon." Kate's smile was friendly.

"Nice to meet you," echoed Sarah, clearly trying on a grown-up manner.

"*Yah*, it was nice to see you all. I hope the quilting continues to go well." Josiah stood as they moved to the door, leaving him and Esther as Hagar showed her visitors out.

As soon as they were out of earshot, he rounded to face the older woman. "Ma'am, tell me who fathered Leah's *Bobbli*."

Hagar's mother looked up at him, saying blandly, "I'm sure I cannot say.

When Hagar returned from seeing out her guests, he turned to her. "Who is the father of Leah's child? You must tell me."

"I cannot understand why you even ask this," Hagar responded, a faint look of confusion on her face. "You should ask Leah, if you have questions. Leah's business is her own business. You know gossiping is not our way."

Frustrated in the face of her response, Josiah got the message. Of course, no one here knew anything about his having courted Leah in Windber. They thought merely that he was a stranger who'd come here with his *Mamm* the year before.

82

To get answers, he needed to see Leah.

*

Perched on a stool in her *Onkle's* 'smithy that same afternoon, Leah watched Gideon skillfully load the red-hot forge.

"You are very adept at that, *Onkle* Gideon," she said, adding frankly, "I'd burn myself terribly."

He glanced over at her, smiling. "I've learned to respect it, *Nibling*. I'm glad you are calming down. Blacksmithing forges are not a place to move about uncautiously. Hagar's *Daed* taught me that right at the first."

Leah got off her stool, wandering over to shift some tools on the work bench.

"Are you glad to be back home amongst your family and friends?" Gideon asked.

She glanced over quickly, "Oh, so very glad, *Onkle*. Everyone has been so welcoming, especially you and my *Eldre*."

"Well, we are very glad to have you back with us, Leah." Her uncle sent her a searching glance. "We worried very much about you. I know this has been a difficult time."

Feeling herself flush, she said, "*Yah*."

Everyone had to wonder at her journey. Although she'd spoken about it to no one, except their bishop, her reappearance in the family way and, then her disappearance into the *Englischer* world after giving birth out of wedlock, naturally had to loom large in many minds. Never had she felt more grateful that talking about neighbors wasn't the way of her people.

It would have been much easier to have lied to the bishop, saying that she'd fallen in with an *Englischer*, a *Schlang* who deceived and abandoned her, but Leah was determined not to be dishonest. She'd sinned in so many ways. She didn't want to add to this. So, she'd told the bishop the truth about the events that had conspired to bring her to this place. She hadn't, though, told anyone Josiah's name. Although she thought about him often— even more so since he'd come to her hometown—she resisted talking about him to anyone. Even Gideon and her *Eldre*.

He could be so silly. The side of her mouth quirked up when she remembered him chasing that silly mare around the pen outside Gideon's 'smithy.

"You and Eli seemed to be doing well," her *Onkle* commented. "I'm surprised you let Hagar keep him for a few hours this afternoon. Your *Mamm* said you hardly let him out of your sight."

"It was difficult," Leah admitted. "I've missed so much time with him, but I know Hagar and you cared for him very well, when I was gone. She loves him, too."

"This is true. I'd guess he'll always have a special place in her heart."

Heat radiated from the roaring forge, making the air in the shop even hotter than the August warmth outside.

Just then the 'smithy door swung open as though pushed hard, slamming back against the wall. Knowing she'd have to face Josiah sooner or later—since he was working here with her *Onkle*, Leah glanced over.

Pausing a moment in the doorway, Josiah stalked in then, his whole body taut, his eyes seeming to burn with intensity. Leah felt herself stiffen.

He didn't even glance over toward Gideon, his gaze locked on hers.

"Leah, is it true? You have a year-old son? We—you and I—have a son?"

Leah abruptly felt frozen, her blood suddenly, startlingly cold inside her despite the heat in the room.

He knew. Somehow, Josiah knew what she'd hidden so ardently.

Peripherally aware that her *Onkle* had laid down his tongs and moved to her side, she was unable to look away from Josiah's stormy face. Her heart thundered so hard in her chest that she ached.

Lips parting to respond, her thoughts raced through the possibilities. She could deny his question, but now that he'd discovered Eli's parentage and the boy's age, Josiah had to realize the truth. He certainly knew she hadn't been with any other *Mann* before him.

She could lie, but Josiah had to know Eli was his child.

Breaking their gaze to throw a wobbly smile to Gideon, she looked back to Josiah. Coming clean seemed, almost, a relief.

"Eli is my son. *Yah.*"

From his place at her elbow, she heard Gideon release a pent-up breath.

Josiah took a quick step forward, a jumble of emotions racing across his face. Shock, anger, vindication...and, just for a flash, joy. The latter was quickly replaced when he said angrily, "And my son. My son, too, Leah!"

She dragged in another breath, unwilling to speak a lying denial she knew he wouldn't believe.

Making herself hold her ground when he took another step toward her, Leah lifted her chin to meet his turbulent gaze.

"*der Suh.* My son! Leah, and you did not tell me." Fire burned in his glittering eyes. "We must marry, you and I. Right away."

"No!" Leah shot back. "No, we won't!"

She was dimly aware that Gideon said nothing all this time. The news that Josiah was the father of her child had to have been a shock to him, but her *Onkle* wasn't her biggest concern now.

Josiah looked at her in incensed disbelief. "Eli is my son. You are his mother. We must marry!"

Josiah glanced at Gideon. "Do you think I can speak to a bishop right away?"

Before her *Onkle* had a chance to respond, she moved forward and grabbed the narrow lapel of Josiah's jacket. "Listen to me! No! I have done things...things I will always regret. I haven't always walked with *Gott.* I let my baby son down for a time, but even with the wrongs I've done, I don't deserve this. I won't marry you! I will not be an...an *obligatory* wife! Second always to your *Mamm*! Married because you had to marry me? No! I will not!"

"Have you lost your senses?" Josiah demanded incredulously after she finished. "You should have told me right away when you knew you were in the family way. Of course, we must marry. Our son deserves this. How could you not tell me?"

Drawing another deep breath, she looked down. "I didn't because—because I knew you'd do this."

"Of course!" He stabbed the air in front of her with an angry finger. "You bore my child. You and Eli belong with me! Of course, we must marry. I cannot believe you kept this from me so long!"

"No," she said again, looking up to challenge his glare with her own. "You refused to marry me before—"

"I didn't! You walked away!"

"—when you declared we had to wait until your *Mamm* was ready to give her approval. I knew then that I deserved better. She will always come first! You showed me that you weren't the *Mann* I wanted to marry."

"That's too bad," Josiah said in a snide voice, "because you carried my son. We must marry!"

This last was made as a proclamation, allowing no further debate.

Leah waved his words aside. "We will not. You cannot make me."

Gideon spoke finally. "She's right, Josiah. You cannot make her marry you."

Jerking his gaze over to the older *Mann*, Josiah said, "Maybe not, but you should convince her, Gideon. You, her *Eldre* or the bishop. She is *narrish* to refuse!"

Her *Onkle* shrugged. "Maybe, but this is Leah's decision."

"Our son deserves to have a *Daed*! Eli deserves this!" The words seemed to explode from Josiah.

"And I deserve a husband who loves me!" Leah felt her cheeks burn. "I do!"

"We'll see what your *Eldre* have to say of this foolishness." With a final retort, Josiah wheeled around and stalked out of the 'smithy.

86

Chapter Seven

The next day, Leah sat in her *Mamm's* kitchen, peeling potatoes for the evening meal. On a nearby rug, Eli rolled and chased a ball. Leah smiled at him, a warm glow of happiness radiating through her. She could never regret Eli.

She'd come home the afternoon before, noting her *Eldre* seemed stunned and hating the significant glances exchanged between her *Daed* and her *Mamm*. She had to speak to them about her bad choice. Josiah must have driven to see them when he left Gideon's forge. Praise be, her parents weren't the kind he'd hoped, not demanding or forcing her to marry him.

To her very great relief, they didn't immediately confront her with his claim, but it hung, crackling in the air.

She supposed there was one benefit to her having run off before. They were clearly aware that this was her business and they'd never demanded she tell them who was Eli's father. In the manner of her upbringing, her right to handle her own business was being respected.

Even if she'd obviously bungled her handling of her business. They were her *Eldre*, however, and she had to talk to them about this.

"*Mamm*…"

The slippery potatoes now in front of her, she knew she had to say something to her *Mamm*. The subject was burning in her chest.

"*Mamm*, I…"

"What is it, *Dochder*?"

Leah struggled to know how to start.

Ever since her confrontation with Josiah, their ugly words had replayed over and over in her mind. It made no sense to keep dwelling on this, as nothing new or brilliant occurred to her, but she couldn't stop thinking about it. After he'd stormed out of her *Onkle's* 'smithy, she'd cried heartily on Gideon's broad shoulders like a weakling.

Trudging home after that ugly confrontation with Josiah, with Eli on one hip, she'd refused to imagine her *Eldre's* reactions to him descending upon them like a fury. Of course, he'd have gone to tell them the truth about her son. She had no question about that. That was one thing about Josiah. He always did what he said.

Along with her knowledge of him, the reality of him telling her *Eldre* was written all over their faces.

The only comfort that had kept her from sinking into a complete welter of remorse was the sweet weight of her son in her arms.

She remembered cooing to him, asking if he'd enjoyed his time with *Aenti* Hagar and she'd reveled in the quiet comfort of putting him to bed.

"You seem…thoughtful," her *Mamm* said now, sending her a quick look. "Is there…anything we need to discuss?"

All through last evening, Leah felt her parents' cautious looks in her direction, seen the meaningful glances they'd exchanged, and had no doubt these were about her. She knew they hesitated to force her to speak of what Josiah told them, but she could only be thankful they were giving her time to ponder what to say.

"I'm sorry, *Mamm*." Leah looked down blindly into the bowl of potatoes in front of her. "I wanted to talk to you and *Daed* about this…but, I've felt so ashamed and so didn't want to…"

Her mother sat silently, waiting for Leah to go on. Her hands busy with peeling potatoes, she kept shooting anxious, concerned glances at her *Dochder*.

"Is…is it true then? What this Josiah Miller said?"

"*Yah*," Leah admitted heavily. Every time she remembered her actions, shame wracked her. She'd been so wrong about him. How could she have been so wrong?

"It is true."

"You met him when you were in Windber?" Her *Mamm's* voice quivered.

"I did."

Rachel was quiet then, as if knowing Leah needed to gather her thoughts.

When Leah said nothing after a moment, her *Mamm* asked timidly, "Is he a…a steady, reliable *Mann*? He hasn't been here working with Gideon long enough for us to know. He seems—"

Leah interrupted. "He is reliable in his commitment to his *Mamm*."

"I suppose this is *gut*."

Shaking her head, she said in a bitter voice, "Not if he insists she come before his *Frau*. Didn't *Gott* say that a *Mann* must leave his parents and hold fast to his wife?"

"*Yah*."

Her chest still rising and falling quickly, Leah lowered a gaze blurred by tears to the bowl in front of her.

Her mother said mildly, "It seems our Fisher friends in Windber mentioned once that the Miller farm is sizeable?"

Drawing another deep breath, Leah said, "*Yah*. He lives there with his *Mamm*."

"Just her? No *Geschwischder*?" Rachel looked confused.

"*Neh*," Leah admitted. "I believe his older brother died in a buggy accident with Josiah's *Daed* when he was small."

"I'm sorry," her mother said with ready sympathy. "That had to be very hard on his *Mamm*, but surely she married again? There were no children from her second marriage?"

Putting down the potato she'd been peeling, Leah said, "No. His *Mamm* never took another husband after the accident. Is there anything else you want to know?"

"I apologize, *Dochder*," her *Mamm* rushed to say. "I don't mean to make you uncomfortable in talking of this."

Suddenly ashamed of her response, Leah picked the potato up again. "*Neh*, *Mamm*. It's not you. I'm just…uncomfortable thinking about what I've done. Ashamed."

"Oh, Leah!" Her mother jumped up from her chair to come around the table and bend to her. "We are all broken and must ask for repentance. All of us."

Tears clogging her voice, Leah said raggedly, "But you haven't sinned as I have."

Her *Mamm* gave a watery laugh, her cheeks damp as she gathered Leah in for another hug. "You do not know all my sins, *Dochder*. *Gott* loves us. Sins are not ranked. *Gott* understands the heart and sees more than we humans can see. Sin is sin. Now, tell me more about this Josiah."

Silence ticked through the shop the day after Josiah confronted Leah about his son. The smell of hot metal filled the 'smithy. Both he and Gideon worked silently with the forge's roar in the background. The only other sound was the clang of hammer on hot horseshoes or the clatter of metal laid aside. In such a noisy environment, their lack of conversation shouldn't have been noteworthy, but it was.

Finally, Josiah blurted out, "Why didn't you tell me?"

His friend stared at him.

Taking a moment before responding, Gideon finally asked, "About Eli?"

"*Yah!*"

With raised brows, Gideon said, "You must be joking. Leah is my *Nibling*. I love her. She asked me not to speak of Eli and I didn't. I wouldn't talk about her hard times with anyone."

Still irritated, he had to say reluctantly, "Of course. I understand."

"Why, when Leah felt she had to leave after Eli was born, Hagar and I cared for the *Boppli*. Eli lived with me."

"Had to leave?" Josiah echoed, knowing he probably sounded peeved.

Gideon lowered the hammer he'd lifted, saying as if he were speaking to a simpleton, "*Yah*. She wasn't here in Mannheim when you came here with you mother, was she?"

"*Neh*." Josiah stared at him, struggling again with the reality that Leah had chosen to give birth as an unmarried *Maedel*, rather than be married to him. It rankled in his gut.

"We were all here then," the big *Mann* next to him continued. "Isaac and Mercy. Enoch and his family. Hagar. And me. No Leah, though."

"Was she back in Windber?" Josiah asked, hoping Leah hadn't returned only to find him off on his mother's crazy mission to seek a different wife for him. "Or was she visiting relatives in some other town?"

Shaking his head with a pitying smile, Gideon said, "Neither."

"Then where?" he asked blankly.

His friend's smile grew more ironic. "Leah said back then that she thought her son would be better off without her."

Josiah swallowed, his mouth suddenly dry. "Without her?"

"*Yah.* She just left for the *Englischer* world." Gideon's voice seemed to reverberate with remembered pain. "For months, we didn't know where she was or even if she was alive."

"I would have married her!" he spit out angrily. "I asked her to marry me before the *Boppli*!"

Tossing aside the heavy gloves worn at the forge, he raked a hand through his hair. "I had no idea. None."

Gideon looked down. "I don't know what happened between the two of you. Leah never even told us who fathered Eli. All she said one time was that she wouldn't be married out of obligation. That I remember. I thought it odd then, but now I understand."

Tormented by the whole situation, Josiah erupted, "I asked her to marry me before Eli was created!"

*

Ada
Windber

The early September sun burning bright above her several weeks after the Pickle Fest, Ada worked in her vegetable plot, trying to loosen a weed. Although the sun shone merrily overhead, a cooling breeze from the north promised that chilly days were not far ahead.

Out of the corner of her eye, she saw Luke standing next to the water barrel near the corner of the *Haus*, his broad-brim straw hat held loosely in one, sun-browned hand, the scooper lifted to his mouth.

Knowing she shouldn't even have noted his presence, she registered his strong neck and throat, the lean stretch of his body—broad shoulders and narrow hips as a bead of water from the scooper trickling down his burnished skin.

Abruptly jerking her gaze down at the hot dirt in front of her, Ada chastised herself for her thoughts. With irritation, she stopped to fan herself. The September sun was suddenly very hot indeed.

For years, Luke had helped her run Abraham's—now Josiah's—farm—as she'd been locked in overwhelming grief. Luke had stepped in as the head farmer until the *Buwe* was old enough to run things himself. She respected the older *Mann* for the steady, level-headed guidance he'd given her son.

Ogling him now was ridiculous. Being alone, after Abraham and little Seth died, had become a habit and should have stamped from her any urge for another *Mann*. That loss was completely shattering and she'd had no difficulty turning aside recommendations to marry again. There had been many. It wasn't a risk she could again run, though. She hadn't thought of anyone but Josiah for a long time, her grief like blinders that kept her gaze focused on only her son.

She knew Luke had lost two wives.

Raising her voice to bridge the short distance between herself and the water barrel, she asked in a matter-of-fact tone, "Will we see you and Mary Grace at the meeting this week?"

"*Neh*," Luke replied in his genial voice, turning to face the garden, "Mary Grace's *Mamm* missed her and asked me to send her home. Abigail is a devoted mother. She thinks nothing of having two *Bopplin* and a little girl to care for. She wrote that Mary Grace should come home."

"Oh, Mary Grace has left already then?"

"*Yah*, back home to Abigail and her husband."

Ada bent back to her task. "That is too bad. I was looking forward to seeing her with you this Sunday. Your *Dochder* must have been glad to have her child well cared for while she was getting situated with her twins."

Luke ambled over to the fence around the garden plot. He leaned against the fence. "I hope so. It was very generous of you to put yourself forward at Pickle Fest to help Mary Grace enter the goat milking contest. I was very grateful."

Feeling herself flush, she sent him a swift smile before saying, "It was nothing, Luke. Mary Grace is a sweet girl."

Luke used a handkerchief to mop his neck before replacing his hat on his head. "She's a determined little *Scholar*, I'll give her that, but she has much to thank you for."

"*Neh*," Ada said to the garden dirt before her. "I should thank you and Mary Grace for our day at Pickle Fest, including allowing me to enter the goat milking contest with Mary Grace."

She glanced up with a sudden smile. "I haven't taught a young child anything since Josiah has gotten to be a grown *Mann*."

"You did a good job. You were very kind to my *Kinskind* and you milked that goat very well," was his jovial response.

Ada dug her trowel deep in the dirt between the rows of fall vegetables, determined to get out the weed, root and all.

"Tell me, Ada," Luke said after a moment, "why will you not let yourself love again?"

Startled at his words, her head snapped around and she stared at him.

"You are a very kind soul. It seems to me that you deserve to mother other *Kinder* and to have more people to love you besides Josiah and that sour *Schweschder* of yours."

"That is a private matter, Luke Fisher. I've long ago spoken to our bishop about the matter. It can be of no concern to you." She'd never had a problem keeping at bay those who wanted to direct her life, but her words now to Luke sounded defensive and excessively prim.

He gave another laugh, easy and friendly. "It is no business of mine. I just don't understand how you can waste all this kindness. Well, I suppose I need to get back to work."

With that, he turned and headed off toward the fields, leaving Ada speechless.

*

Josiah
Mannheim

A week later, Leah snapped, "I don't know why you're even still here in Mannheim. I'm not marrying you."

They stood in the parking area outside the Bontreger's general store, having accidentally—and awkwardly—run into one another there.

He didn't know why her *Eldre* hadn't insisted she marry him, only listening to him with courteous respect when he went to them before showing him the door.

Josiah's mouth tightened, but he just drew a deep breath and seemed to swallow his retort before saying finally, "I told you I came to learn blacksmithing from Gideon. Will you not reconsider and marry me, Leah? Doesn't Eli deserve a *Daed*?"

Jaw tightened, she glared at him. "Eli deserves a lot. So, do I!"

Josiah couldn't think of any response to this.

He paused and, as she turned to stalk past him, he blurted out, "It occurs to me that I don't know much about your life after leaving Windber."

Leah whirled back. "*Neh*. You don't."

Her scornful tone seemed to go all over him, but he swallowed and said, "I wish you would tell me."

When she hesitated to respond, he said in his deliberate way, "I think you owe me that."

"I don't owe you anything!" she retorted in a passionate burst. "Nothing!"

"Not even to tell me of our son's early life?" Josiah said with resolution, "He is our son, Leah. You have admitted that. Will you not tell me of the last year and a half?"

"Eli was cared for! Is that not what concerns you?'

"Cared for by whom? Not you? Why did you leave the *Boppli* with Gideon and Hagar?" Would she tell him? She hadn't been here in Mannheim when he was here with his *Mamm*. Of that, he was sure. Gideon wouldn't lie and Josiah would have noticed her immediately when he was here. "Where were you, Leah? You obviously love Eli a lot. Where were you?"

He didn't know why he needed to hear from her own mouth that she'd disappeared into the *Englischer* world. The reality still appalled him and made him squirm.

Leah glanced aside at two women walking into the store. They were chattering obliviously, just giving her and Josiah a curious look before going inside.

94

She was flushed, saying in a lowered voice, "Not here. You must see that we can't talk here."

As if to reinforce her words, a *Mann* and his *Frau* came out of the general store just then.

Josiah fell silent as they walked past, waiting until the two were beyond earshot to say, "Meet me then. I must know. Meet me under the trees in the field next to Gideon's 'smithy."

She wavered, looking as if she desperately wanted to avoid the conversation.

"You owe this to me, Leah."

As she opened her mouth to probably again declare that she owed him nothing, he interjected, "Think of this as a punishment to me. I let you leave Windber after our fight, knowing we'd shared that…intimate…moment. I followed you here, but I should have done more."

She snapped her mouth shut. After glaring at him for a long moment, she said ungraciously, "Okay. I'll meet you there, but I won't be finished with my chores until later."

"That should be no problem," Josiah responded, tethering his feelings and speaking in his most level voice. "At this time of year, the sun sets later."

"It does." Her words were begrudging.

*

Josiah sat on a fallen log that afternoon in the empty field next to the 'smithy, waiting for Leah. The woodland around him smelt damp and cool. He knew she might not come, having agreed to this to just get rid of him. On the other hand, Leah didn't seem like she was deceitful, even though she hadn't told him about their *Boppli*.

The snap of a twig nearby brought his head around sharply and he jumped to his feet. There she was, the afternoon sunlight filtering through the trees overhead. Even with all that had happened between them, the sight of her still caused his heart to lurch in his chest. She was beautiful with her black *Kapp* neatly pinned to the wings of her blonde hair.

Heaven help him, Josiah only wished time away from her had made him immune to Leah.

"You came." He knew it was a stupid comment, but he found himself saying it anyway.

"*Yah*, but not because I owe you anything," she retorted.

He smiled. "I understand. You came to punish me. Go ahead. Tell me what happened after you left Windber."

Situating herself at the end of the log where he'd waited, Leah didn't respond to this, her jaw set. "You said you had questions."

"*Yah*." He sat carefully at the other end of the log, a half-dozen feet of fallen tree trunk between them. "I—I'd like to know of your life after you left Windber."

She glared at him like he was a beetle on the damp forest floor. "I came home, back here to Mannheim, and I am here now."

"I know you were here for a time, having found you after you left. It must have been hard," he looked up from studying a clump of witch alder shrubbery, "once you…knew about the *Boppli*."

Leah looked away. "*Yah*. It was hard…telling my *Mamm* and *Daed*…and *Onkle* Gideon was hard."

Staring straight ahead, she continued in a hard voice, "Telling them of my sin."

Josiah drew and blew out a deep breath, remorse settling into the pit of his stomach. It wasn't fair that she'd had to confront the results of their sin alone. It was the way of things in this world.

He swallowed, not knowing what to say. Finally, he asked into the silence between them, "They must have asked, wanted to know the name of the *Mann* who took advantage of you. Why did you not say?"

If she had named the father of her *Boppli*, he knew he'd have received a visit from the bishop and her *Daed*. He certainly wouldn't have been welcomed into this town only months later.

"No," she said with scorn. "I told them nothing."

Ignoring the tone of her response, Josiah persisted. "They must have asked. Wondered if you'd fallen in with deceit or harm?"

She was silent for a moment. "They asked if I'd been…hurt or forced. I told them I wasn't. This was my choice."

He smiled involuntarily. "I knew I couldn't have been completely wrong about you. You're truthful. It would have been easier on you to say you'd been forced."

"I wasn't, though," she retorted. "Claiming that would have been dishonest, a sin in itself."

"…and you're not dishonest," he concluded, trying not to sound smug. It was silly to feel this way when she'd been dishonest, of sorts, with him. Really silly. "Did your *Eldre* and your bishop not encourage you to marry…someone? Anyone."

"They wanted what was best for me," she admitted.

"But you did not marry another *Mann*." Josiah would have hated that. His son growing up with another *Daed*. Leah married to another *Mann*, all because she refused to tell him what happened.

Such marriages happened sometimes, he knew, even in a sheltered world like theirs.

"This wouldn't have been fair to the *Mann*…or to me."

Seeing no point in pursuing this, he directed her. "Tell me the rest. Did you stay in your home while you were in the family way or visit a relative elsewhere?"

She looked down. "I stayed here, with those who love me most. My *Onkle* Gideon was a rock."

Josiah frowned. "*Yah*. I don't understand, though. Gideon and Hagar took care of Eli. Why? Were you sick? What of your *Mamm* and your sisters?"

For several long minutes, Leah said nothing, still looking at the ground in front of where she sat on the rough log, her gray-blue skirts spread round her.

"I wasn't sick and my *Mamm* was…very upset. Very. My *Schweschders* are too young to care for Eli alone. Also, *Onkle* Gideon was very insistent on caring for the *Boppli* himself."

Trying to decipher what she wasn't saying, Josiah said, "Naturally, your *Mamm* was distressed for you, but too much to care for the *Boppli*?"

For the beat of several long minutes, she didn't respond. "I was…not thinking clearly."

He frowned, hating that she'd borne their son alone, hating that she'd been so distressed. It was her own choice, though. He stiffened his spirits at that thought. "I would have married you. I wanted to marry you."

Leah's words came back cold. "Not as much as you didn't want to upset your *Mamm*. She is most important to you."

Josiah felt his mouth pull down in frustration. "Should she not be important to me? *Gott* tells us to respect our *Eldre*."

"I don't think *Gott* wants you to cower down before your *Mamm*!"

"I don't cower down!" he shot back. "I'm not less of a *Mann* because I appreciate what my mother has done for me."

"You chose your *Mamm* over me, the woman you said you loved! Is that *Gott's* wish?"

"I do love you!" A tremor ran through Josiah and he'd have snatched the words back, if he could.

Leah stared at him, seeming startled at his rash pronouncement.

He cleared his throat, saying more calmly. "I did love you. I never said I didn't want to marry you, Leah. I wouldn't have— We wouldn't have— If I wasn't committed, you wouldn't have had this rough road. I just wanted to wait…until my mother knew you better, but that would have been nothing, if I'd known about Eli."

Leah drew a deep breath, looking at him a long moment before turning her head to again stare ahead at the brush and low shrubs in front of her. "I left the church. Left Mannheim."

Josiah swiveled around to stare at her, rapping out, "What?"

He knew this from Gideon, but her words still jolted him.

"After I had Eli. That is why my *Mamm* grieved so hard she couldn't function. Why *Onkle* Gideon took Eli to live with him. I left. I ran away."

Shocked more than he should have been, he couldn't move his gaze from the soft curve of her cheek, the beautiful line of her neck disappearing beneath the shoulder of her modest dress. She looked…sad and distressed.

"You…left? Left Mannheim? Left Eli? As a tiny *Boppli*?" Even though Gideon had told him this, the words fell out of his mouth. He couldn't conceive of all she'd been through.

Other than marry him?

Shaken at her words, the image of her, cold and alone in a strange world, ripped across his mind's eye. "You went out? To

98

the *Englischer* world? You didn't...try to harm yourself? Not that."

"*Neh,* not that, but yes. I left him!" The admission seemed anguished, torn from her as she looked over at him. "I felt so evil, Josiah. So wrong and bad! I felt Eli...everyone...would be better if I wasn't...here."

Her mouth twisted as she flashed him a glance. "I thought about hurting myself, but... *Gott* has asked that we never take a life. I think that includes our own. Even though I felt very unlovable...I remembered that He's said He always loves us...and weeps when we hurt."

"Yes." Josiah's response was mechanical and automatic. "*Yah,* that is true."

He shifted to face her. It almost hurt to speak. "You would have done this? Rather than marry me?"

"You didn't really want to marry me!" She flung angrily at him. "Not really. If you'd wanted to marry me, you'd have faced ten disapproving *Mamms*! No concern would have deterred you."

Tears leaked silently down her cheeks as she looked his way, "If you'd really wanted to marry me, Josiah, you'd have come before I left the Haus where I was staying. You wouldn't have taken a week to follow me. Then, when we did speak here after you came secretly to Mannheim and we quarreled so, you just left."

"You are wrong! I did—I do want to marry you!" He shifted closer, the need to comfort her strong in his chest. "I wouldn't have...wouldn't have lain with you, if I didn't. You have to know I loved you. This was not a casual act!"

She shrugged. "Men are sometimes betrayed by their bodies. I encouraged you."

"That is true of both *Menner* and *Maedels*," he retorted, "but not in this case. I was with you because we'd just agreed to marry!"

"If your *Mamm* agreed. Eventually." She sounded scornful again.

Josiah said nothing. He had always sought to be a faithful son, to respect his *Mamm*. Had he used her potential reaction to slow things down with Leah? He just knew he'd felt his head was spinning when he was with her, that his everyday world had slipped away and left him breathless. Without footing.

Had he used his *Mamm* to delay until he'd..adjusted?

He'd even come here to Mannheim with his mother and a matchmaker. Josiah had done that, even though he knew his heart was already given to Leah.

Maybe she was right in being angry with him. Had his response been out of cowardly urges?

His mouth felt seamed shut and he wrestled with the conflict inside him. His *Mamm* had given up everything for him...did that really mean he needed to give up everything for her? To sacrifice Leah and little Eli...for his loyalty to his mother?

He loved Leah. Nothing had seemed right since she'd left him. He'd never regained his footing.

Leah looked over at him, her jaw set now. "I cannot—will not—be a wife of obligation. Not before and not now. I know *Gott* wants more for me. No matter how you push, Josiah, I will not marry   you."

Chapter Eight

The next Monday, Leah clenched her teeth as she sat in the 'smithy corner that was still set up for Eli's use. Her toddler son played on the floor at her feet.

"I don't know why you insisted Eli and I come here," she snapped finally, wishing her *Onkle* would come back into the shop soon to disperse the tense atmosphere between her and Josiah. Even with the boy here, the air between her and the *Mann* she once loved enough to plan a life together was strained.

"I may not convince you to do the best for Eli and marry me, but I insist on the chance to get to know my son," Josiah retorted, looking surprisingly fierce for a normally-calm *Mann*. "Doing it here in this neutral area is better than coming to your *Eldre's Haus* where everything would be even more awkward."

Her son looked up at them uncertainly.

"I'm sure my *Eldre* were very kind to you, particularly given your role in the current situation," she tried to moderate her tone for her little *Buwe's* sake. She didn't want to upset the child. This should have been easier after she and Josiah had talked a little. It wasn't, though, and she wrestled with the urge to snarl at him.

"As I told you, I believe," Josiah said carefully in a dispassionate voice, "our son needs to adjust to his knowing his *Daed*, just as he adjusted when you returned."

"I knew I shouldn't have told you I'd left him," she yelped before forcing a reassuring smile for Eli and moderating her tone. "You just have to throw this back in my face."

Josiah looked annoyed. "I did no such thing."

He looked down at Eli, who had been wandering close in the wobbly manner of toddlers, his face becoming gentle.

"I am glad you came to no harm in the *Englischer* world," Josiah said. "Being there must have been difficult. Particularly without Eli."

"See?" she hissed, struggling to maintain a nonchalant manner. "You did it again. You take shot after shot."

Releasing a deep, long-suffering sigh, the *Mann* across from her said, "You must know that I mean no criticism of you.

The whole situation had to have been very difficult for you. Believe that I see this. Yet, I must be allowed to refer to it, occasionally."

Eli trotted to his *Mamm*, looking at her with concern, his chubby hand on her knee. Leah sent him an encouraging smile, patting his hand. Not for worlds would she admit to Josiah her relief that her young son had lovingly welcomed her return.

"I wish you would not. Let's just ignore that period."

"I do not believe that is possible," he returned in a low voice, squatting as Eli again came close to him. "Hi! Little *Buwe*!"

Watching him finger one of Eli's carved wooden cows, Leah's heart squeezed. She'd once dreamed of seeing him play with their *Kinder*.

Eli lifted a chubby hand to rub his eyes.

Looking over, Josiah said with concern, "Did you not mention that he ate his lunch before coming over? Is he tired now? Most *Kinder* need naps at his age."

With a splash of superiority, she replied, "*Yah*, he will need to sleep soon. He just takes an afternoon nap now."

"You will need to leave with him, then?" Josiah frowned a little.

"*Neh*," she said, demonstrating having learned her son's preferences by gesturing toward a small bed in the corner. "Eli likes being here. The noise doesn't keep him from sleeping. Gideon said Hagar would often have him nap here. In fact, he seems to sleep better. It's strange."

"That's...very unusual. Even with the horses clomping in and out and the hammer strikes on horseshoes from the forge?"

"Apparently, so," she said, as Eli yawned and again rubbed his eyes. "Here."

She reached for the toddler. "He needs his *Windle* changed before he naps."

Josiah guided Eli's steps toward her. "Where are the fresh ones kept?"

She snagged the child as he would have gone after a carved sheep on the other side of his cordoned-off area. "In his *Keavlin* there."

Many aspects of caring for young children were familiar to her, having been helpful with her younger *Geschwischder*. She found the little *Buwe's Windle* and refolded it with accustomed fingers while gently guiding Eli to the floor.

"Here, little *Buwe*," she crooned as he resisted. "We don't want a red bottom."

After a moment of silence, Josiah offered, "Can I help?"

"*Neh*," she said, plopping Eli back while he wailed in protest. "He just doesn't like his play being interrupted. He'll quiet down after a moment."

"You know I can help," he said after a moment, "I may not have had *Geschwischders*, but I cared for my cousins from time to time."

"Okay," she responded, feeling less prickly. She'd always guessed that his only child status was a tender topic. "See? He's accepting that he needs to be changed. He only cried because he's tired."

"*Yah*," Josiah said slowly, studying his son, who no longer protested, but was sucking his thumb.

"We never talked of it much," Leah said, reaching for the dry *Windle* after having wiped Eli clean, "but it must have been lonely growing up alone."

Josiah looked at her before returning his gaze to Eli, now clenching Josiah's fingers in his little fist. "I was used to it. This was all I knew. I can't remember my *Bruder* much."

Inserting the *Windle* pins with practiced ease, she said, "*Neh*, I suppose not, but all the other *Kinder* had *Geschwischder*."

"*Yah*," he said, his expression closed off now. "Most. My *Mamm* had her hands full caring for me and the farm alone."

For a short moment, Leah wondered about his life. She'd been so focused on falling in love with him that she'd not really stopped to think about how different it must have been, growing up without a *Daed*.

The 'smithy door swung open then and her *Onkle* Gideon came in with a big smile. Leah shook her head. She could tell by his goofy grin that Gideon had been visiting up at the *Haus* with Hagar.

He looked recently kissed and she looked down at her son, wishing fiercely that things could have been different with Josiah.

"Your *Daed* broke his leg?" Gideon exclaimed, concern suddenly on his face as he reached out a hand to Leah. "How is my *Bruder*?"

One morning a week later, she stood in Hagar's and Esther's kitchen door, breathing heavily after her hurried walk to tell Gideon of his *Daed's* misfortune.

"He's better now. In less pain, anyway. Ash, our old buggy horse, kicked him when *Daed* was in the barn this morning," Leah clenched and stretched her hands anxiously. "*Mamm* took *Daed* to the *Englischer* health clinic right away. She said the buggy jostling was very painful for him."

"I can imagine," Esther murmured into her coffee cup. Hagar's mother shook her head, clucking in concern.

"I only wish I could have gone with them, but Andrew drove with *Daed* and *Mamm*, since he's the oldest, next to me." Leah paced the kitchen, "I stayed with Eli, of course, and our younger *Geschwischder*."

Of course," Gideon responded. "How bad is the break?"

Leah swallowed, knowing they all remembered Old Abraham, who had lost a leg after being kicked by a horse.

"He's to stay off it for some weeks, but *Mamm* said the doctor pretty much assured them he'd be okay. If he stays off it."

"Of course, Mark will do that! He must not be a cripple. My *Bruder* has always been such an active *Mann*. Why he's always in the middle of every *Haus* and barn build."

Hagar paused in the middle of pouring Gideon another cup, her expression worried. "Of course. We will all take care of his farm, get his crops in. *Gott* has directed us to care for our neighbors."

"*Yah*, although everyone is already stretched, what with Jakob Glick needing help on his farm—"

"And the Bontreger's son needing a new barn for his crops, after his burned," Esther said, grimacing.

"We'll find a way," Gideon said staunchly. "We must. We always help when needed."

104

"Of course, my *Mamm* and we all will help. Andrew is grown—although still a *youngie*. We will manage this."

"You have a lot to manage," Gideon commented, his voice worried. "The crops must be brought in—dang, this is a bad time for me to take a farrier trip."

"It is your business," Leah reminded him. "You must go."

"*Yah*," Hagar stuck in, a worried frown on her face. "Farmers are expecting you to help them."

"Josiah has learned a lot," her *Onkle* added, "but he's not ready to make the route alone and, besides, he's to go back to his farm to help with the crops there."

"And see his mother." Leah's voice was hard. She couldn't help it.

"I suppose. We must find a way." Gideon stated the obvious. "There must be a way to help you through this misfortune. If ever prayer was needed, it's now."

Anxious silence filled the kitchen.

*

Later in the day, Josiah lifted the heavy hammer to flatten the glowing hot horseshoe on the anvil in front him, commenting. "I can't believe your *Bruder* broke his leg. No wonder you're worrying today. Are you sure he's okay?"

He'd come to see Gideon as a *Bruder*, as much as his cousins back home. Having a *Mann* down during the season to bring in crops was never *gut*.

Working at the scarred table a few feet away, a wry smile quirked the corner of Gideon's mouth. "*Yah*. Lots of prayers, my friend. Young Andrew, his oldest son is sixteen, and Isaac, just younger, can help out a lot on their farm, but Reuben's a little bit of a *scholar* still. He helps some, of course, but he can't replace Mark. I'll be leaving on a farrier trip shortly before you're to return to Windber to help bring in your own crops and Leah can't help harvest the crops on their farm as much as Andrew and Isaac will need."

105

"Leah? This is Leah's *Daed*?" Josiah stared at Gideon, laying down his hammer, his concern jolting forward like a buggy with an extra horse.

"*Yah*, she has her hands full with little Eli and watching the younger *Geschwischder* for her *Mamm*. Of course, there will be many others to help as much as they can, but all have farms with crops of their own to bring in. I worry that Rachel and Leah will not have what they need."

Staring ahead into the space over the anvil, Josiah frowned. "*Yah*. You're right. This is very bad."

*

"Here, *Daed*. Let me." Leah took her father's dinner plate a day after he returned from the *Englischer* health clinic with his leg in a heavy, hard cast. "Just sit in that chair with your cast up. We can do this."

The final, long rays of a setting sun could be seen through windows that were half-raised to let in a chilly breeze and the sounds of the evening cicada chorus.

Anna and Grace were clearing the table, with their youngest *Bruder* wiping the worn surface behind them.

"You and your *Mamm*," he grumbled. "I'm not a *Boppli*. If you'd let me, I'm sure I could drive the hay cutting machine."

"*Neh*!" Leah and her *Mamm* said at the same time.

"You must care for yourself." Rachel's brow was creased in concern.

Leah shifted the dinner plate to her other hand, giving her now-free one to her *Daed* to hold as he lowered himself into a chair by the stove. Once he was safely down, she set his crutches to the side.

"You are not to stir yourself," Andrew, her sixteen-year-old *Bruder* entered the conversation, saying stoutly, "Isaac and I will manage fine."

Rachel bent to brush a kiss against the older *Mann's* salt-and-pepper head. "You need to heal, Mark, or the doctor said you could be permanently crippled like old Abraham. We will manage somehow. I'm sure our friends will help as much as they can."

Just then, a firm knock sounded at the front door.

Andrew, the closest to it, opened the door.

Josiah stood outside on the porch, his broad hat perched on his head, a sober expression on his face.

Despite knowing herself to be finished with him, Leah's insides clenched. Before, she'd dreamed of a life when seeing him at her *familye* door would have brought only joy.

Starting forward, her face stiffening, Leah said, "This is not a *gut* time for you to visit Eli. In fact, you should go on back to Windber now."

His solemn gaze shifting from her face to a place over her shoulder, Josiah ignored what she'd said. "May I come in, Mark Lapp?"

Thrown off balance, she shifted forward involuntarily to block her father from him. "This isn't the time to worry him, Josiah. Have you not caused enough trouble?"

Mouth flattening into a line, Josiah bent to look around her, saying again to her *Daed*, "May I come in?"

To her knowledge, the men had not spoken since Josiah had declared himself to be Eli's father. Thankfully, her *Eldre* hadn't pressured her to accept his marriage offer. She had no idea why the *Mann* was here now.

"Come in," her father responded from his chair.

Leah had no choice but to move aside, abandoning her protective stance. Since she felt foolish, just standing by the ajar door, she went to the kitchen, starting to dry dishes as her *Schweschder* washed them.

Although she tried to look disinterested in the byplay between the two *Menner* by the stove, her gaze kept darting in their direction and her ears were strained to pick up Josiah's deep voice.

"Gideon told me of your misfortune." He nodded toward the casted leg propped on the stool in front of her *Daed*.

He snorted in disgust. "If I'd have moved faster, the horse wouldn't have gotten me. As it was, I just caught a glancing blow."

"Old Ash has gotten cranky with his growing years," Andrew commented from across the room.

"He probably misses pulling the buggy," Isaac inserted. "*Daed* has said a hundred times that idleness isn't *gut* for the soul. I'd think it's not gut for horses, either."

"Nice of you to come by before you leave for Windber." Even sitting while Josiah stood over him and, thus, having to look up at the younger *Mann*, her *Daed* managed to hold his own.

Josiah looked down, shifting his feet. "If I could be of service in helping run the farm while you heal, I'd like to help."

Leah's mouth dropped open.

Her dad exclaimed, "I thought you were heading back to bring in your own crops."

"*Neh*, not if I can help here."

"You mean—you aren't returning to harvest your own crops? Your *Mamm* will bear that load?"

"I have a good man that helps with that," Josiah said.

"*Frau* Miller won't like that," Leah said quietly with a smirk, knowing he'd have to strain to hear her words.

Aware that Josiah glanced her direction, she flushed. Her sentiment was vengeful, which wasn't her place, she knew. Regardless, she lifted her chin, staring back at him.

"My farm manager will bring in the harvest," he said deliberately, turning back to speak to her father. "Between them, Luke and my *Mamm* will manage. Here, on the other hand, I can be of service. Let me help."

*

Ada
Windber

The early September sun shone bright outside, but Ada knew the wind blew several shades cooler than it had when her son left. Autumn was approaching and harvest season was right around the corner.

"Have you heard from Josiah?" Luke asked two weeks later, looking up from the bowl of soup she'd made for his lunch that day.

She looked at him, her mouth in a wry line. Matters between them had shifted, somehow, since she'd helped Mary Grace with that silly goat milking contest. In some undefined way, they'd always been linked by their many shared interests and concerns. It was different now, though. She couldn't ignore that he was more of a partner to her. Luke was more—much more—than just a worker on the farm.

She drew in a deep breath.

With anyone else, Ada would have returned a superficial response to the question, turning it aside. The query touched such an intimate matter. Turning it aside with Luke wasn't even a possibility. He'd worked protectively at Josiah's side with her, teaching him to be a *Mann* as would a father. Luke loved her son, she knew.

"*Neh*," she responded from across the simple dining table, "nothing since the quick letter he sent off, saying he wasn't returning for the harvest, as he'd said. Something about helping out a farmer there and knowing you had everything in hand here."

Luke frowned. "Of course, but you've heard nothing more since then?"

Her brow knitted, she shook her head. "I don't know why. He's never gone this long without writing. I know nothing of who he's helping or about the situation there."

"Ada," Luke paused to pass a worn cloth napkin over his mouth, "Josiah is now a *Mann*. He has been for years now."

"I know that!" Her sharp response flew across the table and she glared at him. "I know exactly my son's age."

"Do you?" he said in a bland voice, lifting his brows in question.

"Of course." She knew she sounded irritated. "How could you ask such a thing?"

"Ada, you are Josiah's *Mamm*," Luke said, not unkindly, the smile he sent her full of understanding. "You wiped his chin and taught him to use a spoon. It would be easy to forget he's not a little *Buwe* anymore."

Ada deflated at the gentle note in the big *Mann's* voice. Her sigh was gusty and her mouth quirked in a silent admission that he didn't deserve her irritation. "It's just that I've become...accustomed to...knowing where he is and what he's up to."

Luke sent her a look. "You're accustomed to more than that."

She felt herself bridling at his tone. "What do you mean? I'm his *Mamm*. I raised him myself after his *Daed* died."

"You did." Luke stoically dipped his spoon again into the soup.

"If you have something to say," she pursued with irritation, "just say it."

Without a doubt, she'd have uttered this invitation to no one else. Her own *Eldre* were long deceased and she'd gotten tired of her sister's wintery comments. Inviting comment from others had never been her way. She was glad to have a *Schweschder* live so close, but that didn't mean the woman didn't get on her nerves.

Luke put his spoon down, looking at her steadily. He passed the napkin across his firm lips, setting it down next to his bowl. "Ada, Josiah has been a *Mann* for years now. He runs this farm quite handily now."

"*Yah*, but you still give him much assistance."

"I do," Luke agreed. "Working the harvest without him is no problem. This is my job and my pleasure, since I love Josiah like my own."

"I know you do." She stopped, the look on his face making her bridle again.

"I say this out of understanding and love," Luke looked quite serious and such an unaccustomed expression on his face made her uneasy. "You have meddled in his life. He doesn't need this now."

"What do you mean? Meddled!" The question sprang out of her mouth as a retort and she glared at Luke with irritation. "I do no more than any concerned parent."

"*Yah*, you do," he disagreed in a level voice before picking up again his spoon to dip in the soup.

Ada glared as she waited for him to swallow. "*Neh*, I don't."

"Picking his wife?" Luke asked gently. "This is not the job of a *Mamm*."

"I've not tried to choose Josiah's wife!" she sputtered. "He's doing that himself. Why, when he liked none of the *Maedels* round here, I said nothing!"

110

"You were relieved," Luke inserted amid her sounds of outrage.

"I wasn't!" she insisted. "I know my son needs a help mate and *Kinder*. This is what *Gott* wants for all."

"It is."

"I even found a matchmaker to help him with this. And when he decided the older woman she took us to see wasn't right for him, I didn't quibble or remonstrate with him!"

Luke's response was as even as his gaze. "I believe you were relieved about that."

"I was not!" Hearing her own angry rejoinder, Ada deliberately notched down her tone. "I was not. Why I made no suggestion that he shouldn't go back to Mannheim to study blacksmithing in the town where Hagar lives."

"Of course, not," the big blonde *Mann* across the table said with a smile that set her bristles up again. "You know that she's to marry the blacksmith, Gideon. She's no threat now."

"I'm not threatened by Josiah taking a wife," Ada insisted.

"Ada," Luke reached his big hand across the table to cover hers. "I'm not saying you don't love your son. Just that, maybe, Josiah's not brought home a wife because he..."

Tensing, but not withdrawing the hand under his, she exclaimed, "Because of me?"

"Josiah loves you." Luke reached his other hand over to pick up hers. "If I know you fear him leaving you, he does, as well."

Looking down at her hand, sandwiched between his, she responded in a feeble voice, "I don't."

"Doing so would be natural," Luke continued. "You have made him your everything, since Abraham and your other little boy died. Sheltering Josiah and holding him close. Watching another woman come into his life would be distressing and scary."

"*Neh*." The word came out less convincing than she wanted.

"Sweet Ada." Luke's smile was loving. "You've got to get out of his way and let Josiah know you'll be fine."

"He knows that about me!" She tried whipping up again her anger at his interference, pulling her hand from between his,

111

but his smile didn't waver and she felt the result wasn't really convincing.

"Start building your own life, then. Finally," Luke said steadily. "If you're so sure you don't need to lean on Josiah, go on with your own life. It's okay to love again after losing Abraham and young Seth. You can do it."

"I don't know what you mean." She held Luke's gaze, her words lacking conviction.

"You suffered a tremendous blow," Luke said quietly, his voice sad. "You lost your husband and a child, all at once. It's natural that you'd guard yourself from feeling such a loss again, but you are strong. *Gott* helped you then and He will again."

He took another spoonful of soup. "I should know. He was there for me to lean on in prayer when my Dinah and then later, Grace died. I felt like Job. Like my life would never be *gut* again."

Smiling tenderly at her across the table, he said, "But it was. I healed and…and then came here to work with Josiah. He will be fine. He's a *gut Mann*."

She knew she should tartly assure the brawny *Mann* across the table that she had no doubt about any of this, that, of course, *Gott* was with her, but Ada just looked at Luke without speaking. A tumult of emotion rioted in her chest—regret and fear that she was holding back her beloved son and a mushy sensation in her chest for Luke. She'd felt this before, but the feeling subsided when she breathed and gave it time. Ada wasn't so sure at this moment, though, that she could go on ignoring him.

*

Leah
Mannheim

The September morning sun streamed brightly through Hagar's kitchen window several days later, beams of light stretching across the scrubbed floor.

"We're glad you dropped by on your way to Bontreger's." Gideon reached over to pat the hand Leah rested on the homey kitchen table.

112

Across the room, Hagar bent before the open oven door to pull out a pan of freshly-baked cinnamon rolls.

Leah laughed. "Do you always eat this well?"

She envied the loving look her *Onkle* shared with Hagar. "*Yah. Gott* has blessed me to have this wonderful woman feed me breakfast each morning before I go to my 'smithy."

Hagar settled a plate of warm rolls between them, saying fondly, "You need to keep up your strength to deal with those huge animals all day."

Leah looked down at the table's scrubbed top, seeing out of the side of her eye the smile they exchanged.

"Leah," her *Onkle* said as Hagar moved round to sit on the table bench next to Leah, "you must admit Josiah's stepping up. There are *Menner* who'd have left to go home after figuring out the situation of Eli's birth, and now to help with your *Daed's* farm while his leg heals?"

"I will not marry him!" Leah shot back, both startled and agitated to hear her *Onkle* support the *Mann* who had become her enemy. Strangely. She suspected his offer to help on the farm had some dark motive, but she hadn't yet discovered this. Maybe he wanted to indebt the *familye* to him, try to coerce her to marry him this way.

"Why are you so opposed to marrying him?" Hagar asked in a hesitant tone.

Swinging around to face her, Leah responded, passionately. "Hagar, would you marry a *Mann* who only married you out of obligation? A *Mann* who you know will never put you first?"

Hearing the passion in her own voice, she snapped her mouth shut, her head bent. The other two at the table said nothing while she collected herself.

After a moment, Gideon questioned, "How can you know this? Josiah himself mentioned that he asked you—before Eli—to marry him."

Lifting her gaze to glare at him, Leah tried to keep her voice level. "The two of you have talked of this."

"Well," her *Onkle* hesitated, "He was, naturally, very distressed when he realized Eli was his son and what all the two of you went through without a *Daed* or husband."

113

Leah knew the look she sent Gideon was frustrated. "How well did you know Ada Miller and Josiah when they visited here to look Hagar over?"

Gideon laughed. "I must admit I was more concerned with how Hagar considered Josiah than getting to know them."

Stretching her hand across to table to him, Hagar joined in his laughter before she turned to Leah, to say "I had more to do with Ada and Josiah directly."

"And? What did you think of them? Did he not seem like a Mama's Boy? Doing whatever she wanted?"

Taking a moment to consider the question, Hagar said, "*Neh*. I never saw Josiah that way. Truthfully, he actually seemed nice enough, in a serious way. I did think his *Mamm* was a trial to him, though."

"See?" Leah sent Gideon a triumphant, angry glance. "Any woman marrying him will have an even worse time with Ada!"

"*Frau* Miller didn't seem like an unkind woman," Hagar continued. "Chilly, I suppose, and very concerned with her son, but not mean."

"Leah," Gideon said, his voice level, "I do not wish to upset you, but you must have believed Josiah would be a *gut* husband…or there would be no Eli. You also cannot deny that he's worked hard on your *Daed's* behalf when Mark hasn't been able to work. He didn't return to his own farm, leaving it to his farm manager."

Having shared tender moments and silly ones—chasing after that mare outside Gideon's blacksmithing shop—she stumbled into reflection for a moment. Feeling her neck and then her cheeks flush, Leah said with difficulty, "I—I did believe we would marry."

Her *Onkle* shrugged. "What happened?"

"He declared then that we must not marry right away—he made it clear that his *Mamm* would always come first and she'd have to let him marry me."

"He did?" Hagar seemed surprised.

"*Yah*! It was as though he would do nothing without her approval."

Gideon asked, "Didn't she approve of you?"

114

"Ada Miller has never seemed to know I exist! She doesn't disapprove of me, that I know of, but I'm clearly not on the list of *Maedels* she wants to marry Josiah." Leah felt her mouth firm. "His working on *Daed's* land while *Daed* can't is completely beside the matter. You're right, *Onkle* Gideon. I once believed that Josiah loved me. I wanted to be and planned to be his wife. Only then he made himself clear about his mother."

"You love him still, do you not?" Hagar asked softly, her face filled with compassion.

Feeling the sting of tears at the back of her eyes, Leah pulled herself together, focusing on the simple curtains at the window's edge. She corrected in a firm voice, "I once loved him. I know now that he's not the *Mann* I believed him to be."

"Maybe he is." Gideon shrugged again. "We are not perfect, none of us. We make mistakes."

He reached across the table again. "Enoch and Kate didn't sort through their feelings for one another until after she married another *Mann*. When Jakob Bieler died, they got a second chance to find one another, Enoch has told me. *Gott* knows we human beings are fools sometimes and often need more than one chance to get things right."

"This is true," Hagar returned his clasp, smiling at him. "Gideon and I have had our own bumpy road to finding one another."

"Maybe you should give Josiah another chance," her *Onkle* suggested. "He's still here, despite your rejection, and he wants to marry you."

"You are giving him too much credit," Leah returned, her mouth in a straight line. "You are right, Hagar. Josiah is a serious person about doing what's right. I have borne his son, so he believes we must marry. That does not mean his attitude toward his *Mamm* has changed or that he truly loves me now."

Her hands lay knitted together in a tense ball on the table. "I will not be an obligatory wife, a *Frau* who sleeps in a *Mann's* bed, but doesn't fully share his life. **Gott** wants more for me."

Chapter Nine

"What do you mean the Zook *Buwe* isn't coming to help?" Leah exclaimed a week later, Eli on her hip as she called after her *Bruder*, Isaac.

"He's sick in bed with a colicky tummy or something," her brother Isaac responded, before the kitchen screen door slammed shut behind him.

She followed him out on the porch, going to the top of the steps. "But did you not say that Dan Troyer also cannot help with the harvest today?"

"What's happening?" Her *Daed* hobbled out on to the porch, balanced on his good leg with a crutch under his shoulder.

Torn between not stirring him up and feeling she had to find out the situation with the corn harvest, Leah turned with Eli balanced on her hip, taking the first two steps down to the yard. "It's fine, *Daed*. Go on back inside to Grace and Reuben. They're making applesauce today. You can help with peeling."

Her father looked scornful as he chided her, hobbling over to the porch rail. "Don't refuse to answer me, Leah. I've got a broken leg, I'm not a *Bobbli* to be given easy tasks. Did I not hear Josiah say they were harvesting the corn field today?"

"No," she retorted, refusing to answer his last question, "you are definitely not a *Boppli* because if you were, I could scoop you off that broken leg and take you back inside. You know that Andrew and Josiah are looking after the harvesting."

He glared at her, the corners of his mouth turned down.

"If you are to heal properly and be ready to plant in the spring, you must let us take care of the farm now."

"Your *Mamm* is already helping in the field," her father responded in a tense voice. "She should be the one making applesauce, not your *Schweschder* and your little *Bruder*."

Smacking a frustrated hand against the railing, he made a disgusted noise. "I should be directing this harvest."

She started down the porch steps headed to the corn field due for harvesting before turning to again jog back up them, Eli still clinging to her. "*Daed*, you didn't ask that horse to kick you and break your leg. Bad things just happen sometimes. Now, go inside and I'll find out what's happening in the fields."

Kissing the crown of Eli's head as she stepped into the *Haus*, she called to her sister, "Would you, Anna, Grace and Reuben watch Eli while I run out to where they're harvesting?"

She glanced back at her father. "*Daed* can help keep him amused while you work."

"Certainly. Come here sweet *Buwe*." Her father held out his arms for Eli.

Going swiftly then back out the door after handing off the *Boppli*, Leah trotted back down the porch steps and started down the path to the fields.

The October sun shone warm on her *Kapp*, but she knew the nights were getting cooler as the fall season slid in.

Before she reached the field, she saw her two younger *Bruders* and her *Mamm* next to the rows of tall corn, conferring with Josiah. As usual, the sight of him clenched her insides. She wished she felt less conflicted. It was stupid to dream of a happy marriage to him.

Beyond the small group ahead of her, stretched row after row of the tall stalks of corn, their golden tassels visible in the sun as the wind occasionally rippled across. Two teams of four sturdy horses each stood hitched, docile as they lipped random weeds-- the first team hitched to a corn binder and the second team to the wagon that would be driven alongside to receive the cut stalks.

Leah's steps took her closer to the field as she eyed the crop. Unquestionably, the time of harvest was at hand.

"I can drive the wagon team that trails behind the binder. *Mamm* doesn't need to do this. She can drive the binder," Andrew insisted. "Josiah is tallest and strongest. He should be the one receiving the corn stalks on the other wagon as the binder shoots them to him."

"*Neh*," Isaac protested, "neither you or *Mamm* can handle the wagon team. You've never driven a team of four draft horses and you don't know how to keep them in position. *Daed* always did that with friends to help direct the cut corn stalks on the wagon beside it."

"I've seen him do it a hundred times," Andrew insisted in a stout voice, straightening up as to make himself taller.

117

His younger *Bruder* scoffed, reminding him, "Hundreds of times? You're only fifteen, two years older than me, and the harvest comes just once a year."

Beside the bickering boys, Josiah stood, saying nothing, his expression unreadable.

"I should drive the wagon team, while Josiah catches and pitches back the harvested stalks," Rachel said, frowning anxiously as her sons argued. "Andrew hasn't anywhere near the *Mann* strength he'll have even next year."

Hearing her own voice before she knew it, Leah said, "I think I should be the one to drive the team alongside the binder. *Mamm* can drive the binder, while I handle the wagon that receives the corn stalks Josiah catches from the binder."

All four heads swiveled to face her.

Josiah's face hardened. "*Neh*. You have missed too much time with Eli. You need to care for him up at the *Haus*. We will work this out. Andrew, didn't you say that the *Mann*—Dan Troyer--could come later? And didn't Enoch say he could help in a few days?"

"We can't wait for that," she shot back, glaring at him. She knew she'd missed a vital part of their son's young life, but that didn't change the pickle they were in now. "My familye needs me and I can't ignore that!"

"I can handle the harvest," he said in a stubborn voice.

"Don't think you can boss me around, Josiah," Leah declared, tossing her head. "Even if Dan was to come this afternoon, we'll have missed a day of harvest and we can't have that. The corn needs to be brought in now. We already missed several days, what with *Daed's* accident. We can't wait for Enoch or Abel Schrock to come help."

She'd never have said that where her father could hear her, but it was true.

"What about Eli?" Rachel looked both concerned and relieved to have Leah, not her spindly son trying to keep the powerful wagon team in position beside the binder.

Leah knew Andrew would be taller and more muscled next year. He'd be more able to handle this task. She, on the other hand, was older and could more likely help out in this crisis. She'd driven horses a while now and had worked in the fields a few times with her *Daed* when other help had fallen through for different reasons. She'd actually driven the wagon alongside the binder for her *Daed* the harvest before she'd gone on her visit to Windber.

"Anna, Grace and Reuben are watching him. *Daed* is there, as well. Eli will be fine. Andrew and Isaac are needed to stack the corn stalks the wagon will bring back."

Thankfully, *Kinder* didn't attend school on Saturdays.

She turned to Josiah, who'd fallen silent at her retort. "I've driven the team for *Daed* before."

"The horses are strong," he commented.

"They need to be," she shot back, "for this kind of work."

"*Yah*," her mother said slowly, as if just remembering. "You did drive the team with your *Daed* that one year before you went visiting."

Rachel added, "I drove the binder for Mark when we started our farm and, although that was years ago, I can certainly do it now."

"It's settled, then," Leah said, knowing she was more likely to have the strength to drive the team than her younger *Bruder*. "I will drive the wagon, while Josiah stands in it to receive the stalks on the wagon. You—Andrew and Isaac—can help unload the wagon when needed."

She whirled around to Josiah. "And you are not to be a hero and stick your fingers in the binder—if it gets jammed—for many have lost digits that way."

At her preemptory direction, he began to grin.

In no way responsible for the *Mann's* fingers, although she knew that was what he was thinking, Leah blew out an exasperated breath. "For we need no more wounded *Menner*. Besides, you wouldn't be able to help as much while *Daed* heals. We can't have you unable to help, too."

His grin widened. "True and the farm is the most important thing."

"That's right!"

"Not my fingers," he said, drawing his lips together as if restraining another smile. "Okay, Leah. I'm sure you can do this. We should get started on the harvesting."

"*Gut*." She turned to mount the wagon.

"Rachel," he directed, "you get the binder team lined up to start cutting the stalks. Leah and I will follow close by and I'll throw them when they come out the binder."

"*Yah*." She started toward the binder.

*

While the others lined up the wagons, Leah raced up to the *Haus* to arrange for Eli's care, before she then ran back along the path to the corn field.

The smell of large warming draft horses rose to her as she neared. The big horses stood docile in their harness, accustomed to this work.

Then she vaulted up into the driver's spot, standing up with the horses' reins clenched in her hands.

"Are you ready?" Josiah called, looking back over a shoulder from his spot in position to receive the corn stalks.

"*Yah*," she said, readjusting the leather reins in her hands.

The sun hot on her head, she braced herself and, as her *Mamm* slapped the reins against the broad backs of the draft horses, Leah started off her own team. Back and forth they went over the corn field, Leah trailing a horse-length beside the binder wagon that cut the stalks and sent them up a shoot. Out of the corner of her eye, Leah saw Josiah stretching to catch the cut stalks, scooping them over to lie on the flat wagon bed she drove. His fixed jaw, visible under the shade thrown by his broad hat, indicated his concentration on his task. She'd seen her *Daed* do this job many times, but seeing Josiah in this act was…too….

Heck, she wished she didn't notice the flex of his strong body, the way he easily lifted his armloads of stalks onto the growing pile on the wagon.

With fixed concentration, she focused on the ears of the horses she drove. Their pace was steady, the binder ahead to the side.

Just in front of her wagon, *Mamm* drove the binder, it's sharp blades slicing through the tough corn stalks at the base before the stalks were sent up the shoot from which Josiah caught them. The steady plodding of horses' hooves mixed with the crackling whirring sounds of the blade slicing the stalks and the crunching of the wagon wheels over the corn stubble.

It was a scene she'd witnessed many times over the year, the harvest coming with the seasons and vitally important to the financial health of the family. That's why they had to take care of this for her father. Only a girl raised on a farm could appreciate the significance of harvesting a field that had been carefully tended through the growing cycle.

The midday September sun shone hot on her black *Kapp* and she reached down several times to drink from the covered mug at her feet. Her arms and back ached from her task, but she wouldn't complain if it killed her.

As was often the case, the binder slowed several times.

Daed always sharpened the binder blades before harvest every year and she'd heard him mention to her *Mamm* having done it again that season before his leg injury. The binder still got stuck sometimes, though.

She tensed every time Josiah jumped from the wagon to reach under it to pull stalks free of the blades. Getting a hand anywhere near those blades involved risk. She knew doing this in the field meant reaching blindly under the bulky machinery.

Stopping at the end of a row, as *Mamm* guided her team to pivot around to start the next section, Josiah ran an eye over the field. "We've done a good third of it, I'd say."

"*Yah.*" Leah wiped at the water on her lips, returning the mug to sit at her feet.

Realizing her hands tensely clenched the team's reins, she shifted them to allow herself to stretch her fingers a moment. This working beside a *Mann* with whom she had such a tangled past scraped at her nerves.

Continuing on through the warm and sweaty morning, there were only several more strips of corn field to harvest when the binder wagon again slowed to a stop as a loud grinding sound came from the machinery, stalks no longer shifting up the chute.

"I'll have it clear in a moment," Josiah said, dropping again off the wagon to walk over to the binder.

Leah raised her eyes to the blue, blue sky, trying not to see him drop to his knees to again reach under the dangerous binder. This time, she heard him grunt loudly and found herself swiveling back to unwillingly gaze at him kneeling in the stalk stubble beside it. Watching him yank and yank at a stalk that was clearly bound tight, she glanced at her mother. *Mamm* had also turned anxiously in her standing position on the binder, guiding the team into each new section of the corn field.

They both knew the danger, the friends who had lost fingers doing just this.

Josiah leaned in further, his head and shoulders disappearing under the binder as he fought to free the stalk.

Feeling her heart in her throat as the sun streamed down on them, Leah's mouth tightened. This was ridiculous! Time seemed to lengthen and grow taut as he wrestled vegetation from under the contraption. Every incident in which a friend or relative lost fingers in farm accidents loomed hideously in her mind.

"What are you doing, Josiah! Get out from there," she finally yelled.

"In a minute. I almost have it."

The machinery groaned just then, a horrendous shriek that her made jump. Her jaw tightened. She said with a snap, "Are you going to be under there all day?"

"Leah!" Her *Mamm* made a shushing sound.

Ignoring this, Leah added in an irritated voice. "Maybe you should get out from under there."

The binder groaned again. What could be seen of Josiah's body tensing as he yanked at the stalks keeping the machine from moving.

From under the binder, his muffled voice said, "If I can just—"

Another shriek of metal rent the air. Tilting her chin upwards to the sky, Leah could only imagine his fingers bloody and dangling. She'd watched her *Daed* hone the razor-sharp binder blades. Farm equipment could be horribly risky.

"Stop!" she demanded in a loud voice. "We can flip the binder over and pull the stalks free. Be smart here!"

"Leah," Rachel said again with despairing notes.

Glancing at her *Mamm*, she said in a sharp voice, "You know that it has to be cleared that way sometimes."

Another groaning of metal from the binder had her drop off the wagon and stalk over to where Josiah's legs extended.

"Josiah! Stop being a *Dumm hund*! The binder needs to be flipped!" Her words were sharp with anger, images of him with a mangled finger in her head.

At that moment, Josiah could be seen backing out from under the machinery.

"*Gut!*" Her fear and relief drove her to add, "Finally, you're being *schmaert*."

He pulled himself out and straightened to his feet, a gnarled corn stalk in his hand.

"*Denki*. That's nice of you to say." His expression bland, he turned to Rachel. "You can drive on. You'll find it works now."

Going back to the wagon Leah had driven while he tossed armloads of stalks on to the flat bed, Josiah jumped onto it in a lithe move and turned to extend a hand to her. In a level voice, he said, "We'd better get moving if the wagon's to be close enough."

Staring resentfully at his hand, anger and huge relief wrestling with some unidentified emotion in her chest, she finally put hers in his and let him tug her up to his level. In a low voice she knew only she could here, he said, "I know how to be safe, Leah. I've run my own farm—and harvested corn—for years now."

Tears pricked behind her eyes as she made her way blindly to the front of the wagon. None of this should have mattered to her. *Gott* had told them to care for one another, but the intensity of frustration and distress in her seemed out of line with this commandment.

Rachel started the binder forward again and Leah guided the team of horses to follow closely, so Josiah could again start catching the stalks coming out of the chute. Looking back at him doing this, stretching to shift his armloads of stalks to the back of the wagon, she couldn't not see the way his shirt clung damply to the muscles in his back. Every time he reached up, grabbing an armload to toss back, she saw the flex of his strong back.

Turning back to the team, Leah gripped the reins, reaching to swipe at a tear that trickled down her face.

*

123

Finishing his lunch under a tree several hours later, Josiah chewed slowly, his gaze brooding on the mother of his son, several feet away. Leah sat fanning herself in the sliver of shade thrown by the wagon, looking slender and too young to have a child. Hot and sweaty, too, as they'd been working for hours.

She'd never looked more beautiful to him.

Josiah looked away, not able to sort through the chaos in his mind.

As Leah's *Mamm* and two brothers were gone to take the teams of horses to drink from a nearby stream, just the two of them sat there in silence.

He still didn't know how to wrap his mind around all that had happened between them. The burst of pure happiness he'd felt when she agreed to marry him two years ago. The burn of passion and love that had led to Eli coming into the world. It was all a blur he couldn't untangle. Except the passion. He remembered that clearly.

The situation had played out very differently than he'd expected. He'd been so wrong to act as he had. Insisting that they wait to marry? He must have lost his mind.

They'd shared their moments and Leah had brought the golden time to a horrible end by rejecting what had seemed at the time like his simple request that they delay their future long enough to let his *Mamm* adjust. It had seemed like such a small thing. He'd never even considered there might have been a consequence beyond his broken heart. So stupid of him.

His jaw tightened. Josiah had grown up without a *Daed*. Eli wouldn't do the same. Somehow, she had to be convinced to marry him and bring his son back to live on the farm in Windber.

"Is your sandwich good?" he asked in an awkward attempt to break the silence between them.

"*Yah*. I suppose." She looked over, her expression so stubborn it made his heart ache, while at the same time he wanted to cross the short distance between them, yank her to her feet and kiss her senseless. Maybe that was the way to accomplish his purpose.

He loved her and he liked thinking she loved him, too.

Josiah swallowed a groan.

He had to have been *narrish* back then, to let her leave without considering the possible situation they'd created. Only a crazy *Mann* could have ignored that particular likelihood.

Looking blankly over the wagon, he again silently asked *Gott's* forgiveness. Josiah should never have let Leah leave, regardless. How could he have been such a *Debiel*? Although he knew *Gott* loved him even in his foolishness, and forgave him his errors, he just couldn't forgive himself.

When he thought of the hardships Leah had faced… Never mind that she could have returned to him and he'd have married her instantly. Gladly, married her.

Still.

"I'm sorry," he blurted out.

Leah look over at him. "What?"

"I said I'm sorry," he repeated in a low voice, his head bent to stare at the soil. "I should have been there for you when Eli was born. I should have been your husband. I was stupid not to think this could happen. You faced all this alone… You shouldn't have had to face being in the *familye* way all alone. The terrible stress of it. It's no wonder you thought everyone would be better off if you left."

At her silence, he looked up to meet her gaze. "I'm so glad you came back. I-I couldn't have lived with myself if I were part of separating you from your home. From your *familye*. From *Gott*. Although I believe He was always with you."

"Oh." It was her turn to look down. "That was my doing, Josiah. I was the one who ran away."

He responded forcefully, "It was understandable, with everything you faced."

Shaking his head, Josiah added, "You should never have had to face it alone! I should have been here."

"Maybe. *Yah*," she said finally, "but to be fair, you didn't know of Eli's existence. I didn't tell you."

"You shouldn't have had to tell me," he says shortly. "I should have known."

Bending her head again, Leah said with apparent difficulty, "*Gott* has forgiven you. We are told He forgives us all, if we accept it."

He dropped down to sit beside her in the shadow of the wagon.

"I do accept His forgiveness...but I'm having difficulty forgiving myself for this."

She made a sound, both scoffing and understanding at the same time. "As if our requirements for forgiveness are greater than His. We are silly."

Her expression drooped in sorrow.

Giving her a long look, Josiah agreed, "*Yah*, we are."

"I know the struggle to forgive one's self for something that seems unforgivable." Her deep sigh made him turn toward her.

"My sin was greater, though," she said in a low voice. "You didn't know of Eli's birth...but I did. I cannot plead ignorance. I had the sole care of a tiny infant. Me. Just me. My son. My son!"

The word seemed wrenched out of her. She looked up, her blue eyes wet. "I left him, Josiah. I'd given birth to him! And I left him to my *Eldre* and my *Onkle's* care."

There was such pain and remorse in her face. He ached to pull her into his arms and hold her. Josiah longed to give her any comfort he could...but there was too much between them. As if she were old *Frau* Wickey from Windber, he awkwardly reached over to pat her hand.

"*Neh. Gott* knows. He sees the heart and He knows what a terrible situation you were in. Just as he forgives my stupidity."

"This doesn't excuse me! How could I have done this?"

Josiah blurted out the only thing he could think. "You have suffered. You missed out on caring for him when he was very small. I believe God understands and forgives you—that is His promise. He loves us, even though we are flawed, but we still must experience the results of our actions. In this world."

Wiping at the moisture that had leaked onto her face, Leah said, "*Denki* for that."

"Please," he continued, fearful of shattering the tenuous kindness between them now, but compelled. "Please marry me, Leah. Eli is my son. I promise to love you both with all my heart."

"More than your *Mamm*?" she blurted out.

This again. Not sure what she meant, what she expected, he hesitated for a moment. "I don't know what you mean. My *Mamm* is my *Mamm*. I will always love her, but that doesn't mean I can't love you and Eli. Marry me."

Her expression hardened. "I cannot. You know why, Josiah."

*

Ada
Windber

Later that week, Ada rose from the ground in her garden patch, brushing the dirt off her apron. Surveying the rows of vegetables lined up in front of dark leafy greens mixed with medium tones. The red tops of beets peeked out above the soil surmounted by erect green tops.

The rattle of a farm wagon mixed with the sounds of steady oxen driving up from the fields. So intent on watching the crew come in, Ada didn't, at first, notice her sister's buggy pulling to a stop outside the *Haus* she shared with Josiah.

Judith pulled back on the reins, the woman's face almost as long as that of her horse.

Giving her garden-grubby hands one last dusting on her apron, Ada left the garden, walking over to greet her *Schweschder*.

"*Goedemorgen*, Judith," she offered as she came close. "I didn't expect you to come visiting this morning."

"Didn't myself expect to come," her sister responded, sounding as grim as usual.

"Oh?" Ada waited for the other woman to explain herself. Judith was a very regimented person. A deviation from her schedule was unusual.

"I thought of you when I was on my knees with *Gott* this morning. Thought I'd better get my concerns off my chest." She finished tying off her reins.

"Oh," Ada responded without enthusiasm. As the elder sister, Judith's concerns had always carried the weight of parental edicts.

127

Having finished pouring some water from the rain barrel into a bucket for her buggy horse, she crossed the small lawn before Ada's *Haus*, climbing the porch steps with agility normally seen in individuals half her age.

Following her sister up the steps, Ada scoured her brain to think of what she might have done to earn her sister's disapproval.

Judith sank into a porch rocker, producing a fan from somewhere and began to vigorously move this to and fro before her face. "It's ridiculous to be this warm in September."

"*Yah,*" Ada said mechanically, sinking into a rocker next to her visitor. It was silly to be this concerned about how she might have earned Judith's censure.

"I have," her *Schweschder* said in majestic tones, "said nothing as you've raised Josiah, although others have not hesitated to advise you about the matter."

Her senses already perked, she noted Judith's acerbic tone as she said the last part.

"What concerns you?" No use trying to dodge this. It was better to get right to it, if her sister had something to say.

"I've been, of course, conscious of your situation, after Abraham and Seth died."

Ada took a deep breath.

"You were, naturally, grieving for quite some time. *Mamm* and *Daed* worried about you. We all did."

She said nothing, remembering the dark despair that had gripped her for a long time.

"Can you still remember what their voices sounded like?" Judith looked at her with compassion. "My own *Boppli*, Lucas, died when he was only four days old, you remember, and I worried that I'd forget the exact sound of his cry."

Looking down at her lap, Ada nodded. "I remember. That was why I stayed with you so often after the accident. I knew you understood."

"I did." The grimness in the older woman's face seemed more pronounced. "Your situation was worse than mine, though, this is hard to imagine. You lost both Seth and Abraham, at the same time."

Ada reached out to briefly clasp Judith's hand before withdrawing hers.

"We go on after loss, however. You had to concentrate on raising Josiah. I had my other *Kinner* and Hiram. It doesn't make the losses easier, but maybe this keeps us from shriveling up to nothing."

"*Yah.*" She didn't know what she'd have done without Josiah. He'd been her rock, him and prayer. Her reason for going on.

"It is the most bitter of losses," Judith said, "to lose those we love to death, even though redemption offers us hope."

"*Yah.* It's just hard to deal with this world."

Her sister nodded.

They sat, rocking in silence for several moments.

Finally, Judith stopped, turning to face her. "My understanding of your grief is what makes what I have to say now even more difficult."

Having stopped her own rocker, Ada told her sister, "Just spit it out, Judith. What do you have to say?"

Her sister's smile was both bleak and appreciative. "I've always liked that you get right to the point. This is it, *Schweschder.* We cannot allow loss to make us afraid to live."

Ada threw up a relieved hand, scoffing, "I am not afraid. Why do you say this?"

"In general," Judith sounded even more grim, "you face up to everything. You can be a formidable woman."

"Then, what do you mean?"

Judith said nothing for a moment. She then raised her gaze to Ada's face. "You've never married again."

"What do you mean?" Ada repeated, although she knew very well what her elder sister meant.

Starting her rocker, her face stern again, Judith said, "You haven't taken a second husband after Abraham."

"I was busy," Ada retorted, "raising my son and managing this farm. It's not small, you know."

"I am aware, but you know a new husband could have helped you with this. Abraham's farm would have been palatable for many."

She bent a stern eye on her sister, "But your son and managing the farm, this is not why you've stayed single."

Ada fell silent.

"You've been afraid. Afraid to lose again, afraid another *Mann* and child will die on you. Josiah is grown now, though, and no longer needs your watchful eye. It is time you risked again, *Schweschder*. This life involves both love and loss. You cannot do one without the other."

"That may be true, but there is no *Mann* who I want to marry. Do you think I haven't looked around? That this has never occurred to me?"

Her sister smiled, an amused, but not heart-warming expression. "Are you sure there is no Mann for you? Seems like your farm manager smiles at you often and I've heard you laughing with him. No, you've been too afraid to go down that road again. You have tried harder to find Josiah a wife than anything near the effort you've made to look for a husband for yourself."

Staring at her sister for a moment, Ada said finally, "Of course, I am most concerned with my child."

Judith's expression turned wintery. "You taking another husband would be in your child's best interest."

"What do you mean?" Ada knew her question was defensive.

Sidestepping this entirely, her sister abruptly asked, "How is Luke Fisher doing? He's always such a friendly *Mann*. He's been a good addition to our community."

Ada felt her gaze narrow. "Why do you ask about Luke? I know what you say about him smiling at me, but that means nothing. He's fine, I believe."

"He's been here quite a while now, helping you run the farm Abraham left for Josiah."

"*Yah.*" Still riled by her sister's comments about marriage. "This has something to do with me marrying again?"

Although she'd meant her response to be calm and amused, she ended up uttering a pugnacious question with her jaw thrust out.

"I have," her sister commented in a meditative voice, "been watching this Luke Fisher."

"Watching him?" Ada asked suspiciously.

"I believe he has feelings for you."

130

"What? No! You're wrong." Rejecting the idea immediately, she eyed the older woman even as a little voice whispered in her head. Ada shoved it aside.

"He has not married another," Judith commented.

"Luke was married twice and both wives died. He has grown children." Ada had a sudden, jarring image of him with a new *Frau*. It was startling how she instantly disliked the imaginary woman.

"He is," her sister said with a sly smile, "a healthy, attractive *Mann*. Very pleasant, too, particularly when you're around."

"That's just his way. Luke gets along with everyone."

"Does he?"

"Yes, he does." She prayed for *Gott* to help her settle down and not explode all over her smirking sister. "You're wrong, Judith."

Her sister began waving her fan languidly. "But beware, sister, a *Mann* like him will not wait forever. He'll marry someone eventually."

Ada made a disgusted sound, starting to rock quickly. "Well, it's nothing to me. He's welcomed to marry whomever he likes."

"*Gut*, sister, because I think he likes you."

"Don't be silly," Ada snapped, hating that she didn't hate the image her sister's words brought to her head. She didn't want to marry Luke. She didn't care who he married… Really.

*

After her sister left later that day, Ada went out to give the chickens their evening feed. The coop was situated behind the *Haus*, a few yards from the big barn. In the paddock beside the barn, a stack of baled hay stood broad and tall. To her frustration, Luke was working there, braced about three bale levels high.

"*Goedenavond*, Ada!" he called out with his usual smile, climbing up several more levels.

"Hallo," she responded, hating that she'd blushed at the sight of him. Drat Judith.

131

His shirt sleeves rolled up to reveal sinewy forearms, a broad-brimmed straw hat on his head, Luke looked vigorous and strong. The gray that threaded through his beard was that of an older *Mann*, but he looked better than he had any right to.

She hated noticing him—more now, she insisted to herself—that her *Schweschder* had made such a big deal of Luke.

He didn't have romantic feelings for her, Ada was sure of it! In spite of this, she found herself replaying moments when he'd smiled more warmly at her than at others... His fervent gratitude when she'd entered the goat milking contest...

Ridiculous! Ada scolded herself. Of course, Luke had been grateful at that moment. He'd have been grateful to anyone who got him off that hook.

"*Hallo!*" he called, his silly grin widening. "We got a lot of bales from those hay fields, don't you think? It should bring a tidy amount."

"*Yah,*" she snapped, irritated with herself. "Is there a reason you're standing on that pile of bales?"

Luke grinned again. "I certainly can see from here. By the way, the roof on your Haus looks good."

"*Denki,*" she responded dryly, "but you don't need to be up there for that."

"What?" he said, venturing near the end of row of bales so high she had to tilt her head to meet his gaze.

"Come down from there," Ada commanded, irritated that her annoyance mingled with anxiety as he went closer to the edge. "You might fall and you're needed to run the farm!"

"And you don't care if I am injured," he teased, "as long as I can work?"

To her frustration, he teetered playfully ever closer to the edge.

"Come down, you *Schaviut!*" She tried to swallow the fear in her throat. "You're acting like a *Youngie* and you should know better!"

"Oh!" he cried out, faltering back and disappearing over the edge.

He was there in front of her and then gone.

"Luke!!" Ada cried out anxiously, dropping her pan of chicken feed to dart around the high stack of hay bales.

Her long skirts swirling, she rushed around, terrifying images playing in her head of his broken, mangled body on the other side at the base of the hay bales.

And there he was! Healthy and whole. A laughing Luke standing on a row of bales just below where he'd acted as if he'd fallen.

Stopping as she careened around the stack, she cried out, "Oh! You *Debiel*!"

Pressing her hand to her heart, heat prickled across her cheekbones and, for a moment, she felt lightheaded. Never having passed out in her life, Ada thought this might have been what it felt like.

Angrier than she thought she could ever be, she snarled out again, "You *Debiel*!"

Apparently, realizing that his prank had nearly scared the life out of her, Luke lithely dropped down to climb off the stack of hay bales, his face now concerned. "I'm fine, Ada. Truly. I was only joking. I didn't fall."

Her heart still thundering in her chest, Ada smacked away the hand he'd extended as if to catch her in a fainting fall.

"Get away from me!" she gasped out. "Never do that again! Do you hear me? I will have you thrown from this farm!"

"I'm fine, Ada. Truly, I'm fine." His contrition was visible. "I never meant to frighten you."

"I cannot—" she gasped, "I cannot!"

Whirling away, she muttered, "I must leave."

Ada ran then, her long skirt clutched in her hand. Her cheeks wet with tears that blurred her vision. Crossing the yard, she fled into the Haus, slamming the screen door behind her. Back to the wall next to the door, she sank to the kitchen floor, her fists against her mouth, wrenching sobs wracking her body.

Images of Abraham's broken body mingled with pictures of Luke's tangled limbs at the bottom of the stack of hay bales. Luke, laughing and golden. Luke who had been in her life all these years, sharing guardianship of her son.

Fresh tears tracked down her face.

She couldn't do this again. Grief and terror and bitter, bitter loss.

Not again.

She'd survived losing Abraham and Seth. Caring for Josiah had given her strength, but she was older now and she didn't think she could survive losing another love.

*

Leah
<u>Mannheim</u>

A week later, the sun slanted low in the sky above as Leah and Josiah walked in from the far corn field. She drew in a breath and said abruptly, "You're a *gut Mann*, Josiah."

He looked over, a broad hat casting shade on his face, as he continued to walk across the stubbly field with her. "Why do you say that? It seems you've had a very different opinion of me, up to this point."

Wishing, not for the first time, that she could read his expression, she said in a clipped tone, "You've really helped my *Daed*—us all—with the farm since he broke his leg."

They continued together, puffs of dust rising from the drying field with each step they took.

"I'm glad to have made a difficult situation better," he said finally.

Responding to an urge she didn't want to examine too closely, Leah said, "You were to travel back to Windber, to your farm. How did your *Mamm* harvest your crops there?"

It was petty of her to feel competitive with Josiah's mother, but some wicked little part of herself rejoiced at having won the contest this time. Heaven knew she hadn't won before.

Despite this, Leah immediately sent up a prayer, asking for *Gott's* forgiveness. They were to turn the other cheek, when struck, and Ada Miller wasn't the one with whom she'd argued.

Sliding a sideways glance at the *Mann* walking beside her, Leah acknowledged to herself that although she had reason to hate Josiah, she couldn't. Particularly now, when he'd worked so hard this last week to help her injured *Daed*, ignoring his own crops for theirs.

"How did your *Mamm* fair, with you not there to harvest your own fields?" She looked over at him again. "She must have been upset."

"Possibly."

The strong line of his jaw was somber when she again peeked at his profile.

"It must have been difficult for her." Trekking beside him across the field, she knew she should shut up about this, but images of her enemy suffering sat uncomfortably in her head.

The sun behind him as it sank to the hill tops, Josiah turned, looking her full in the face. "Of course, it was hard to leave my crops to others to harvest. You must know why I did this. Why I left this to my farm manager and my *Mamm*, instead of dealing with it myself."

Bristling a little, as much because of her own guilt at having rejoiced in Ada Miller's situation as at the tight anger in his voice, she glared at him.

"It was your own choice," she said in a defensive voice. "No one made you do this."

As he'd stopped near the edge of the field, her steps ceased, as well, as they stood tensely facing one another.

Again he said, his words taut, "You must know why I did it."

Sucking in a breath, she said, "*Neh.* I do not know. We are told to help our brethren, but not if that means ignoring your own business."

A frustrated sound came from his throat.

"You, Leah, make me so angry sometimes." Josiah closed the short distance between them, hauling her into his arms. He lowered his lips to hers and kissed Leah rigorously.

Shocked, she made no resistance to his sudden action, quiescent in his firm embrace. Within only a few seconds, his kiss gentled, becoming soulful and filled with longing.

Without meaning to, Leah melted against him, softening. She knew this kiss. Knew the natural, clean smell of his skin, the feel of his arms around her. Suddenly, she was there again—in love with Josiah Miller and eager to give him her heart.

Then, abruptly, the kiss ended and he was several feet away from her when Leah blinked her eyes open.

135

"I'm sorry. I shouldn't have—"

Finding her voice suspended, she said nothing.

"Is there nothing I can do, Leah," he finally uttered in a low, tight voice, "to show you I never meant things to go so wrong between us?"

With those words, he turned and clomped off into the next field leaving her stunned and frustrated and filled with confusion.

Leah watched Josiah's strong back retreating into the next field, her heart thumping painfully in her chest. His kiss...oh, that kiss.

She still loved him.

The truth of it burned in her head, as if the words were outlined by fire.

She still loved him, even after all this. There was no denying it.

Stumbling forward to settle onto a fallen tree at the edge of the field, a pool of her long green skirt settling around her, she felt dampness trickle down her cheeks. Her tears dripping down to the high neck of her bodice, Leah prayed for *Gott* to help her. He had to   know   she   needed   it   now...

Chapter Ten

"*Mamm*!" Josiah exclaimed the next day, his abstracted frown lifting as he stood in the buggy sweep outside the Stoltfus *Haus* where he'd stayed while working with Gideon.

Ada descended the buggy, a familial, comforting presence in the very calm, almost bland expression she wore.

Jerking himself out of his abstraction—everything inside him hummed and wrestled with the memory of kissing Leah—he put a smile on his face and wrapped Ada Miller in a welcoming hug. "I didn't know you were coming. Is all *gut* with the farm? And with Luke?"

The sun had sunk to just above the tree-fringed horizon and tangle inside him after his interaction with Leah sat heavily on his mind. He'd loved her initial, quivering response to his sudden, unplanned kiss, but that didn't mean anything was truly changed between them. Would she come to him? Finally become his *Frau*?

"Son!" His mother hugged him, pushing back to examine his face with what he recognized as an anxious, clouded gaze. His *Mamm* wasn't easy to read, but he knew her well. Well enough to know when something was troubling her.

As frustrated and distracted as he was with his own mess, it seemed she must have registered this, but she seemed preoccupied herself.

"You've not written recently," Ada said. "*Yah, yah*. The farm is fine. Are you okay?"

The rigid line around her mouth made him frown. This seemed to be about more than his turmoil.

He answered slowly, "I'm good. I've just been busy helping Leah's *Daed* harvest their crops, since he got hurt. I must go back to help more tomorrow. You say all is well with our farm? Luke harvested our crops without any problem? That new hay field is bigger than we usually sow."

Ada Miller's mouth seemed to tighten more. "*Yah*, the bales were harvested and bound."

"*Gut*. I am glad to see you." Josiah shifted to walk her into the Stoltfus *Haus*. "Come in. I think *Frau* Stoltfus will have a bed for you. Her one *Dochdar* is visiting relatives in another town."

"Oh, good."

He didn't think he'd ever seen his *Mamm* so distracted.

"And Luke is well? He has everything on the farm in hand?"

"Luke is fine, as far as he can be," she snapped. "Why you have a *Debiel* for a farm manager, I don't know."

Answering slowly, Josiah said, "Luke is not a moron, *Mamm*, and you first hired him to manage the farm when I was just a Scholar."

"*Hhmmmph*!" she nearly growled as she subsided with a thump into a rocking chair on the Stoltfus porch.

"Are you and Luke arguing?" he ventured.

"*Neh*! As if I'd even bother with the likes of him!"

Josiah stared at her, remembering several moments between his farm manager and his *Mamm*. A twinkle of understanding glimmered through the morass in his head.

Ignoring her unkind, uncharacteristic words, Josiah sank into a rocker next to hers. He reached over and patted her hand. "Luke isn't a moron, *Mamm*. Has he done something to upset you?"

For the first time he could remember, Ada Miller burst into tears.

*

Leah
Mannheim

Slipping into a seat for worship at the Stoltfus Haus the next Sunday with Eli on her hip, Leah adjusted his *Kevlin* to be out of the path. Bending forward to do this, she took the chance to quickly glance around the crowded meeting for Josiah. She knew he was staying here and knew, too, that he came to every Sunday meeting.

Scanning the crowd as she straightened in her chair, Leah's startled gaze fell on Ada Miller, sitting directly across from her. Right next to Josiah.

His *Mamm* was here.

138

Although she knew it was *narrish* to think this way, Leah couldn't help the crazy thought that Josiah's *Mamm* had somehow learned that Leah had born her grandson. It made no sense that Ada somehow knew that Leah had been wondering, in the last few days, if she shouldn't surrender to her love for him and give in to Josiah's demand that they marry.

Crazy of her to wonder if Ada had come to insert herself into the situation.

Her body suddenly as stiff as a tree trunk, Leah absently patted Eli's warm little back, staring angrily across at his father. No matter whether she loved him, it didn't appear anything was different.

Nothing. His *Mamm* was still between them and he'd only be marrying Leah out of obligation.

Josiah hadn't sought her out in the meeting—as would be appropriate in a *Mann* who had found the woman he wanted to marry. He hadn't brought his *Mamm* over to introduce her to Leah, now that the woman was here.

They sat on opposites side of the room.

Nothing had changed.

Leah wanted to cry.

Later that same day, as Eli napped on his small cot, Leah sank to her knees beside her narrow bed. In silence, filled only with the sound of the little *Buwe's* even breathing, she began to pray.

The quilt on her bed soft under her clasped hands, she opened her mind to her Creator.

Help me, Gott. Help me know what is best. What should I do? I love my son with all my heart. For his sake, should I enter a marriage with Josiah, in which his Mamm will always be first? I know You love me. Do you think such a marriage would be gut for me? Josiah can't love me with anything reflective of Your love— love me as You've said a Mann should love his wife. What should I do?

Rising to sit on the bed later—it felt like she'd been in prayer for hours—Leah realized she'd been tearfully hoping *Gott* would direct her to give Josiah another chance. It was wrong, but she'd wanted promises from *Gott* that what she secretly craved doing would all work out in the end. Josiah would love her and their child, placing them first in his heart behind *Gott*.

It wasn't fair to expect this, she knew. *Gott* was always with her, watching over her and her little *Buwe*, but that didn't exempt her from using the sense *Gott* gave her.

Josiah continued to demonstrate that matters were the same. He didn't truly love her.

*

Josiah
Mannheim

The fall morning dawned bright the next day, Josiah made his way along the road to Gideon's smithy. He still didn't know what had happened between his *Mamm* and Luke. She'd refused every attempt he made to discover this. He wished he could help—he loved Luke like a *Daed*—but he could do nothing if nothing was said to him.

As to Leah, his reflection had decided him, and he'd decided to again press her to marry him. He loved her and he always had. He thought her response to him—saying he was a *gut Mann* and then quivering in his arms—all this told Josiah she still loved him, too. Having her as his wife was his greatest desire. Leah and little Eli.

He would go to her and again profess his love.

Josiah strode along in the crisp air, the sun just rising over the rim of trees around him. The road firm beneath his feet, an occasional bird singing in the trees overhead. Each gust of wind sent leaves falling to carpet the road beneath his feet.

All the sudden, Leah tumbled down a slope from the wooded area onto the road in front of him.

Her sudden appearance stopped him in his path.

She stood, arms crossed, six feet in front of Josiah…glaring at him.

Startled, he exclaimed, "Leah!"

140

Their last interaction had held that tender kiss. His heart ramped up, despite her expression. She loved him.

"I see that your *Mamm* came running to protect you!"

"What?"

Her forceful, angry words made no sense to him, but he had the normal, male response, caution immediately descending.

"Your *Mamm*." Leah stalked a pace forward. "I saw she was with you at the service yesterday."

"*Yah*?" He drew the word out, not sure how his mother being here mattered.

"And once again," she said scornfully, "you are choosing your mother over what you say you feel for me."

Confused, he frowned. "Why would you say that?"

Ignoring his question, she spat out her own. "Did you tell her about me? Or Eli? Did you say you'd found the love of your life? The woman you would, finally marry?"

Josiah quirked the side of his mouth in annoyance. "You have said—many times—that you will not marry me."

"And you know why!" She dashed away a tear that glittered on one cheek.

"Leah," he said in a gentled tone. "Why are you so upset?"

He'd thought, with her telling him he was a *gut Mann*, that they were moving beyond this hostile place.

"Why am I upset!" she echoed in a shrill voice, seeming even more incensed by the question. "You have not told your *Mamm* about me! You didn't bring her over at the service to meet me. You gave no indication of even knowing me! You haven't told Ada about Eli, have you?"

He stiffened, feeling the blood drain from his face. "No…not yet."

"I knew it!" Her words sounded both triumphant and sorrowful.

"She just got here," Josiah rushed to say, feeling a little defensive, "and she's got something on her mind. I wanted to let her rest and then talk with her. Today. I planned to talk to her today."

He tried not to sound angry, but Josiah knew that was his tendency when at all upset.

"*Yah*, of course you did." She turned, as if to walk away.

"Leah, I love you," he blurted out, his world tilting. "So much. You must know that! I've helped on your family farm, leaving my own harvest to others. Just to be here for you. I love you and Eli."

She glared at him, tears now tracking down her face. "*Neh.* You just feel you should do your duty. I was wrong to ever believe you. To lie with you. I was wrong. Goodbye, Josiah. Have a good life."

*

Stalking into the 'smithy a few minutes later, Josiah slammed the door behind him,

From where he stood, stoking the forge, Gideon looked up, his eyebrow flying up in a comical expression. "*Goedemorgen,* young Josiah."

"Good morning," Josiah snapped.

Putting down the tongs, with which he'd been rearranging the coals in the forge, the older *Mann* said, "What ails you this morning? You've certainly never shut the door so loudly."

"That woman—that *Nibling* of yours!" In his frustration, Josiah's words came tumbling out without his normal measured tone. "One day she kisses me like she could eat me up and then, the next day, she accuses me of—of betraying her!"

Gideon's eyebrow rose higher and a smile tugged at his mouth. "I assume we're talking about Leah?"

"Of course," Josiah retorted. "Who else?"

"I have no idea who all you're kissing." Pressing his lips together, as if resisting a smile, Gideon shrugged.

"It's as if she wants me to shun my own mother! To throw her out of my *Haus* and never see her again! Didn't *Gott* say we are to honor our *Eldre*?"

"Leah wants that? You to throw your *Mamm* out of your *Haus* for her? She told you she wants that?" Gideon seemed unmoved by Josiah's unusually dramatic claim.

"Not in those words," he admitted, still fuming, "but that's what she meant! I've never chosen my mother over Leah! Not

142

ever. Not really. I may have gotten...confused at the beginning...but I've not put my *Mamm* before Leah."

Gideon looked up from his work at the furnace, no laughter in his face now. "Ever? And Leah thinks you did? Why?"

Ready to shoot an answer back, Josiah paused, snapping his mouth shut.

Had—had it truly seemed to her that he'd placed Leah behind his loyalty to his *Mamm*? Probably. Questions rioted in his head. Was that what he'd actually done? Before, when he'd asked her the first time to marry him? It certainly hadn't seemed that way.

"Regardless of all that happened between us before, I never meant to choose my mother over Leah." he said in a more moderate tone. "That was never in my thoughts,"

"But Leah might have felt that way?" her *Onkle* asked.

In the act of tying on his leather apron for blacksmithing work, Josiah looked down at the strings. Private things were private. This subject was uncomfortable for him, even with Gideon, who he'd come to see as a friend.

Josiah had never been one to talk about his business. Even more than most, he felt uncomfortable spreading himself out for all to see. Gideon knew only the bare outlines of everything between Josiah and Leah.

"I don't know what she thinks," he said, "except that she's now decided I am a *Schlang*."

Turning to place a horseshoe in the forge, his blacksmithing teacher said, "I'm guessing it's not that bad. You are definitely not a snake."

"I love her," Josiah said in a low voice. "I love Leah, but I won't shun my own *Mamm* for her."

With a long steady look, Gideon commented, "Leah's heart is kind. I don't think she would ask this of you. She wouldn't hurt a fly, much less anyone you care for. Perhaps the two of you need to talk this out more clearly. You both seem to be upset, right now, but I'm guessing a more middle ground solution would be *gut* with the both of you."

Josiah gave him a long stare, his mind grappling fruitlessly to find a solution that would bring Leah happily back into his arms.

"I don't know how to talk with her. She's angry now that I didn't bring my mother over to introduce her at the meeting."

Gideon shrugged. "Have you told your *Mamm* about any of this? About Leah...or Eli?"

"*Neh.*"

"Maybe you should," the other *Mann* said in a mild voice. "Why would you not?"

"I don't know," Josiah said slowly. "I'm just—I take care of things myself."

Looking at him, Gideon said nothing.

"Only this," Josiah added after a moment, "this isn't just about me, is it? I need Leah and, I guess, I need to act like I need her. Like...she's important to me—her and our son."

Chapter Eleven

The room shadowy around them as evening fell that evening, Leah sat in her living room, lit sparsely by the light from one oil lamp and the glow from the fireplace at the end. Her father occupied a chair to one side while her *Mamm* had gone to settle down the one of her *Geschwischder* who was still awake.

Leah and Eli had been assigned the only other bedroom on this level, next to her *Eldre's*, and she'd left her door cracked, in case her sleeping son woke and cried out.

Soon, they all would head to bed, farmers rising early.

The lamp sat on a table closest to her *Daed*, his casted broken leg sticking out before him as he sat with a book that was spread on his knees. Leah knew he often read about crops and farm matters.

She sat, staring into space, with a small half-finished shirt on her lap, destined for Eli's use, once she'd finished it. In the way of little *Kinder*, he grew like a weed.

Josiah's face loomed in front of her mind's eye despite her efforts to direct her mind into less complicated channels. He'd looked so surprised when she confronted him angrily and had, then, gotten so defensive when she'd challenged him on his actions since his *Mamm* showed up.

Sniffling back the moisture suddenly clogging her nose, Leah picked up the shirt fabric, holding it up to the lamp's light with determination. She wouldn't cry anymore for him, having already wasted too many tears for Josiah's sake.

It was no use repining or wishing things could be different. He'd made his choice, both before and now. No matter what he claimed, her little *Buwe* and she weren't first on Josiah's list. The thought sent a piercing shaft of pain through her and she shoved it aside. She'd spent too many months—almost lost her *familye* and her faith—running from the reality of her situation. It didn't matter that she—she loved him. She loved him, but Josiah clearly didn't love her in return. Not really.

Even in His scripture, *Gott* had said they were to leave their parents and cleave to one another.

Dropping her hands again into her lap, Leah couldn't push away the thought that maybe she should consider his marriage proposal, for Eli's sake. Wouldn't it be better for her son to have his *Daed* at hand? Maybe that was more important than her own needs.

Staring into the slumbering coals in the fireplace, she again considered this view of the situation, clenching her fingers in the folds of shirt. It wasn't the first time she'd circled around this possibility. All through her pregnancy, she'd wrestled with wondering if she should sacrifice herself for her child. She'd again and again revisited *Gott's* words, reading again how much He loved her and wanted the best for her.

Why did it have to be this way? To seem as if what was best for her son wasn't best for her.

"You might be best to put that sewing aside for now," her *Daed* finally commented, his voice humorous.

"What?"

His words jerked her back to the current moment and, dazed, she swiveled her head toward where Mark Lapp sat on the nearby couch.

His expression gentle, her father closed the book he'd been reading. "You have a very expressive face, Leah. I don't think your mind is on your sewing."

Her vision blurred again as tears filled her eyes, she made no answer.

"I don't know what to do, *Daed*," she whispered. "Josiah says he wants us to marry, to make a home for Eli…"

"But?" her *Daed* asked comfortably.

She didn't know how he could be so calm. Didn't *Eldre* want their *Kinder* to be righteous?

"You and *Mamm* must want me to marry him." Leah echoed aloud her dilemma. "I know I've grieved you both greatly and you probably wish me to do this, if only to give no one reason to remark on my situation."

He rose ponderously from the couch, using a crutch to keep his weight from his broken limb. "*Dochder*, your *Mamm* and I are so very grateful to have you again in our loving arms and again attending *Gott's* services. We are relieved to have you here."

146

"Thank you, *Daed*." Her voice was husky with the urge to cry again.

He hobbled the few steps to her chair. "*Gott* loves you. Leah. He knows your heart is as important to your son as married parents. Whatever the issues between you and Josiah, marriage to him must not be a sacrifice to you. It is a gift to have a partner by your side. I want you to have this."

"I love you, *Daed*," was all she could choke out past her emotions.

"And I, you, *Dochder*." He bent to kiss her head through her dark *Kapp*.

How many times had she felt the press of his affection there on her head? She wanted to cry even more.

"Don't stay up too late," he admonished, hobbling toward the room he shared with her *Mamm*.

"I won't," Leah choked out.

Despite her promise, however, she sat staring into the cooling fire for quite a while, wondering what to do.

She loved Josiah. She couldn't deny that. Despite their trials and twisted path, she loved him. Should that be enough? Shouldn't that make her willing to take a back seat to his mother in his affections?

*

"*Mamm*," Josiah said the next day when out for a walk with his mother, "sit down here in the sun. I want to talk to you."

"Of course." Ada sat on a rock in a shaft of sunlight that fell through the trees beside the trickling stream.

The setting was beautiful, the foliage around the creek already showing signs of fall, bright yellows and russets in the leaves that had already fallen on the path. Several floated along on the rippling water flowing past.

He cleared his throat. The time for this conversation was long past, but he still felt the need to circle around it.

Tucking her gray skirts under her neatly his mother smiled up at him as she had a thousand times. "Your room here seems comfortable. Is the blacksmith, Gideon, a *gut* teacher?"

147

"*Yah*, very *gut*," Josiah responded briefly, "but that is not what I wanted to speak to you about."

Thoughts shuttled through his head and, not able to decide how best to bring up the topic that had to be addressed, Josiah veered into another area that had been on his mind.

"*Mamm*, why did you come to Mannheim? You knew I was coming home soon."

"*Yah*, you said that in your letter." Her smile was moderate and seemed, to Josiah anyway, somewhat strained.

Abruptly, he asked again, "Then why did you come here, *Mamm*? I am certainly glad to see you, but we agreed you would stay home, watching after the farm. I am well enough here and would have come back to Windber already, if Mark Lapp hadn't broken his leg and needed my help on their farm."

Ada Miller didn't respond, her face going even more blank as she visibly swallowed.

"Did you and Luke have a falling out?" He didn't even know what made him ask the question. His mother and his farm manager had always worked together cordially enough, keeping his farm together and both sharing in the raising of him since his own father had died. They'd acted like…partners.

Swatting at a nearby weed, his *Mamm* said irritably, "I'm sure Luke is fine. He doesn't need me to handle the farm. He does well on his own."

Josiah's gaze narrowed in confusion. "Do you—do you want him to need you?"

He'd never given it much thought before, but it struck him now that his *Mamm* and his good friend were much the same age and that he'd sometimes—absently—noticed that Luke was particularly cheerful when Ada was around.

"No!" Her response was adamant, especially for a woman so calm and in control, most of the time. Ada smiled with obvious effort, saying more coolly, "*Neh*. Luke is fine, I'm sure, as is the farm. I just wanted to see you."

"Okay," he responded, staring at her a moment before his gaze dropped. He couldn't put off any longer the conversation that he should have had—well, he accepted now that he should have told his *Mamm* right away when he first proposed to Leah.

Much trouble would have been avoided and, he recognized now, his *Mamm* would have accepted his marriage. She only wanted him to be happy and Leah made him happy…when she wasn't making him nuts.

"*Mamm*," Josiah said abruptly, "I love a girl. I should have told you this several years ago, when I first met her."

"You're in love? Several years ago?" His mother questioned, seeming surprised. "In love with whom?"

Breaking into an involuntary smile, Josiah responded, "With Leah Lapp. You know I've been helping on her *Daed's* farm just recently, after he broke his leg."

"Oh? I don't understand." Ada seemed a little dazed. "You met this Leah here in Mannheim?"

"*Neh*." He said, owning his guilt fully. "*Neh*, not for the first time. That's why I said I should have said something to you before."

Looking back up at Ada, he said, "I need to tell you the whole thing, *Mamm*. I've been a fool. An utter fool."

His mother smiled faintly, patting his hand, "I doubt it, but tell me all about it."

"I met Leah first several years ago in Windber."

"In Windber?"

"*Yah*. I met her there when she visited. You may not remember her, but I fell in love with her then."

"You've loved this girl all this time?"

"All this time."

"*Yah*," he admitted.

"All while we were looking for a *Frau* for you? Traveling around with Sapphira Schwartz, the matchmaker?"

"*Yah*." Remembrance of that time erased any urge to smile. "*Yah*. Two years ago, I proposed to Leah and she accepted me."

"You proposed?" Ada exclaimed. "How could I have not known this? Why did you not tell me?"

"*Neh*, I didn't tell you," he said heavily.

As if she were putting together a puzzle, his mother murmured, "No wonder you found no other girl to marry."

A frown knitted her normally-smooth brow. "Why didn't you tell me about her?"

149

"Because Leah and I had a falling out," he admitted. "Right after deciding to marry. And then she left Windber for home."

He drew in a long breath, letting it out slowly, the memories threatening to flood him.

"You argued and didn't make up? This does not sound like you, *der Suh*," Ada chided. "You're not one to argue. Why, there have been moments when I thought you should have gotten angry about different things and you did not."

"I know." His smile felt grim. "I tend to be even-tempered in most everything, but…I wasn't in this. I told her we had to wait to tell you about our marriage. I think I felt…nervous and…rushed. I foolishly thought we needed to wait a year to—to let you get to know her."

"Me? What do I have to say to this?" Ada looked mildly surprised.

"Much, I thought. You and I have always been close."

His *Mamm* nodded. "This is how *Gott* would have *Eldre* and their *Kinner*."

"True…but in this case, I put my worries about you ahead of Leah." He swallowed hard, ducking his head in shame. "We'd already…acted as if we were married. I—I was stupid."

Josiah brought a fist slamming down on his knee. "I should never have done this!"

"I guess I haven't…been the best mother," Ada admitted. "I—I have held you too close, not really urged you to find a *Frau*, despite my attempts in that matter."

"You are the best *Mamm*," he responded sharply. "The mistake was mine."

"You can be bullheaded," his Mamm commented after reflecting a moment. "And not easily led, despite my silly attempts."

"I must admit, he said with the shake of his head. "I love Leah very much, but only with her do I get…do I argue this way. She makes me so *narrish*. I hate feeling that crazy. I love her, though, more than I'd ever thought I could. I very much want to marry Leah."

To his surprise, Josiah found talking about this openly brought a wash of relief, mixed with his other feelings.

150

Ada laughed suddenly. "Your *Daed* and I used to have some very heated conversations."

Her expression shifted then and she abruptly fell silent.

"I must tell you the rest," Josiah said finally after a few minutes. "I have been an idiot. Leah and I were to marry—to be a *familye*—and I, for the first time I got..."

"What?" his *Mamm* demanded. "There's more you haven't told me?"

"Yes." The word felt heavy as it came out of his mouth. "I got caught up in the moment with Leah and... We..."

Ada started shaking her head. "Son, you didn't. What am I saying? Of course, you did. You are very much a *Mann*. You said you'd acted as if you were married."

"I'm not *Mann* enough." Josiah said, "Although I didn't know it, Leah was in the *familye* way with my son when she left Windber."

Gasping, his mother stretched out her hand. "She had your child? Without a husband?"

"*Yah.*"

"Poor girl!"

"I cannot say how much I regret letting her leave," he said heavily. "I was stupid and—and worried that you didn't know her well. Or, at all. I told Leah then that we needed to wait to say anything to you or her *Eldre* about marrying."

"You did this because of me?" his mother demanded. "Am I so exacting? So hard to please that I would reject the woman you love?"

He felt heat crawling into his face. "I said I was stupid. I was new at all this. I'd never loved before...and I wasn't thinking right."

"*Neh*, you weren't." Lifting her brows as she spread her hands, Ada said, "I am surprised Leah didn't marry another husband here."

"Her *Eldre* suggested she do that, of course, but my Leah is very determined."

"Your Leah?" his *Mamm* said with amusement.

"*Yah, Mamm*, if I can convince her to marry me." His voice firm, he added, "I love her, *Mamm*. I always have."

Ada laughed.

151

"You aren't sure of convincing her to marry you? I want to meet this girl," she said abruptly. "She sounds strong-headed herself. We apparently have much in common."

*

Ada
Mannheim

Later that same evening, Ada smoothed down her night dress in the flickering light of a single candle, mulling over everything Josiah had said.

He loved a girl.

And had a son.

In bemusement, she sat back on the edge of her narrow bed, glad of the quiet and privacy of the room she had been allotted here at the Stoltfus farm where her son had been housed while in Mannheim.

Josiah had found the woman for him…and he had a *Boppli*?

It still confounded her.

He wasn't her little *Buwe* anymore. That was clear. That Josiah had a son outside of marriage surprised her massively. He wasn't stuffy, but her son was usually such a rule follower. She knew he could be playful at times with those closest to him, but Josiah was made of stern moral fiber.

Yet, he had a child and wanted, naturally, to marry the mother of his son.

A smile stretched across Ada's face.

If this Leah could be convinced to marry him…

Searching through her memories, Ada tried fruitlessly to pull up a visual of the girl her son loved so much, having asked her to marry him and then going against his own nature to make a child with Leah. It embarrassed her that she couldn't remember her son spending time with any particular girl two summers ago. What was wrong with her that she had been so out-of-touch?

Her smile fading, Ada stared into the shadows and asked *Gott's* forgiveness. Had she been so...disconnected? So absent in her own life? So ignorant of her son's interests?

Luke would say so. The thought whispered through her.

Without meaning to, she let pictures of him muscle into her thoughts. He'd always been there. Managing the farm for her son. Always cheerful and ever-present.

When had she gotten so accustomed to his presence that she couldn't envision him not being there? She'd even entered a public goat-milking contest for him!

Running her fingers lightly through hair that was, for the moment, unconfined by a white *Kapp*, she frowned and tried to remember Abraham's smile, the sound of his voice. It had been so long... He'd been gone—along with their firstborn son—so long. Not a day went by when she didn't miss the boy and her husband, but somehow in the years, the ache had somehow settled, had become less piercing when she breathed.

Refusing for so long the calls to remarry, others had stopped pushing her to do this. She'd been adamant in refusing all suitors. After all, it wasn't uncommon for a *Mann* or *Maedel* to never marry. It happened. Sometimes. True, she'd never wanted this for Josiah.

The jolting moment when she'd thought Luke had fallen from the hay bales flashed again in her head. Somehow, she'd found herself weeping over and over since then. She couldn't say why.

And now this with Josiah.

Ada blew out her solitary candle and lay back in the narrow bed. Wisdom should come with age, but apparently that wasn't automatic. She felt unsettled and confused and she didn't know what to do with herself. For so long, she'd defined herself as Josiah's *Mamm* and nothing more, but Josiah was a *Mann* now, a father himself, and she didn't know where that left her.

*

Leah
Mannheim

Two days later, Leah sat in Hagar Hershberger's cozy kitchen, her hand wrapped around a mug of coffee. Being here was calming and helped distract her from the dilemma in front of her.

"I'm sure it will be *gut* to be married to Gideon, after all this time. Only a week until you're married! Why the two of you have known one another your whole lives!" She smiled at her friend.

"*Yah*," Hagar said, sitting across the table, an errant wisp of blonde hair escaping her *Kapp*, "but most of our friends have known their eventual mates most of their lives."

"True," Leah admitted before observing, "but most haven't had the history you and Gideon share. Why you two have been enemies for years!"

"Not enemies," Hagar murmured, her cheeks becoming rosier.

"Oh, come on," Leah laughed, "you almost left this *Haus* because your *Mamm* deeded the 'smithy in the back to Gideon."

"Well, he was in the wrong to tell my beau not to marry me," was Hagar's spirited response.

Leah said, "Gideon was right in thinking Peter Schwartz wasn't the right *Mann* for you. Gideon is the right *Mann*!"

"Yes, he is," Hagar grew even rosier, "and, it will be wonderful to be married to him, at last, but he still didn't have the right to stick his nose into whether or not Peter asked me to marry him."

Leah shook her head. "What if you'd said yes and married the wrong *Mann*? Knowing the right thing to do can be very confusing."

"Like with you and Josiah?" Hagar inserted with a sly smile that held no condemnation.

"Yes," responding with a heavy sigh, Leah looked into the murky liquid in her cup, thinking her future sometimes was as unclear.

Hagar got up to smooth the blue skirt of the dress she and Leah had just finished. "This is a nice dress for the wedding. I'm sure I'll get many years of service out of it."

"*Yah*, that's a nice blue on you, too. It's *gut* you look so well in that lighter shade." Leah took a sip from her cup.

154

Wheeling around to face her friend, Hagar said, "I know the past several years have been hard on you, Leah, but I think I understand Josiah's actions."

"You do?"

Hagar straightened the blue dress where it hung and came to sit down across the table. "I—I was mixed up about Gideon. I didn't understand why he said what he did to Peter, all those years ago, and I've been angry, even distrustful of him since. We didn't talk about the things we should have talked about. It seemed too hard and—and useless. We should have, though. Truly. I think you and Josiah have things you haven't talked through."

"Maybe," Leah sighed, "but his choice of his *Mamm* over me is clear."

"It could just seem that way," Hagar argued. "Has he talked about why his *Mamm* and he are so close? I know, I feel very close to my *Mamm*. Closer than most. These past few years of just the two of us in this *Haus*, she's felt like my best friend. Maybe you and Josiah need to talk about how things have been between him and his *Mamm*."

"What could he say that would make his actions different? As plain as day, his choice was clear when he said we had to delay our marriage until his *Mamm* approved." She knew she sounded scornful, but she couldn't help it.

Hagar looked doubtful. "He actually said those words? Just like that?"

"Something very close to that," Leah insisted defensively. "How am I supposed to remember two years later the exact words he used?"

"I'd think those words would be burned into your brain." Hagar commented in a mild voice.

"His intent was," Leah said firmly.

Her friend leaned forward, stretching a hand across the table to touch her own. "Was this not a—a fragile time for you? Forgive me, but you'd become closer to Josiah than any *Mann* in your life. You'd taken one of the biggest risks a woman can take. Eli is proof of that."

Silent for a moment, Leah lifted her gaze, saying in choked words, "I was so stupid. It didn't feel like a risk, at the time. I trusted in Josiah completely."

"And then he said something that seemed to flip over your world." Hagar sent her a compassionate smile. "At the same time, doesn't Eli deserve a *Daed*? And you a husband to stand by your side?"

"Would Josiah be that, though?" The question spilled out of her and she looked at her friend through a film of tears. This dilemma tore at her. "I have been over and over it, Hagar. *Yah*, Eli does deserve a *Daed*—"

"Who lives with him," interjected the other woman.

"*Yah*, who lives with him, but I deserve a husband who will stand by me. You're right! I deserve that. I just don't see Josiah choosing to do that, even though *Gott* directs us to leave our *Eldre* and cleave to our mates!"

"I guess this is the conflict," Hagar said slowly. "Give Eli what he deserves or insist on what you deserve."

"*Yah*." Leah brushed away the wetness on her cheek.

"I still think you and Josiah need to face this and talk together. What is *gut* for your son cannot be bad for you. Otherwise, it truly wouldn't be best for Eli…or Josiah."

Looking at her friend, despair flooding her thoughts into mush, Leah said, "I know you speak the truth, I just don't know what to do with it."

*

The Tuesday morning of her *Onkle* Gideon's marriage to Hagar Hershberger began clear and crisp.

The Lapp cows had been milked in the early morning darkness and all the farm animals fed in the dark long before dawn. At six thirty, Leah kissed little Eli goodbye and got into the buggy, adjusted the blanket over her legs in the morning cool before she clicked to the horse to start off.

She, along with Sarah Beiler, Abigail Hochstetler and Anna Lehman were to be Hagar's wedding attendants. As the female *Newehockers*, they were arriving early at Hagar's to help her and her *Mamm* prepare breakfast for them all. As *Newehockers*, they were eager to be ready to welcome the many wedding guests that morning.

Leah directed the buggy horse by rote, thinking about what was ahead. That Hagar and Gideon finally found one another was a gift from *Gott*. She didn't, however, look forward to taking part in the emotional moment while feeling Josiah's gaze on her.

Why didn't she know what to do? Had he changed? He now promised to put her first, to love her in the truest sense of the word. Could she trust him?

If he were different, wouldn't he have brought his *Mamm* to meet her?

She'd believed they'd have a very different future when he'd asked her the first time to marry him. Certainly, she'd believed they would have gone through their own marriage ceremony by this time.

She knew that Enoch and Kate Miller, along with Enoch's *Bruder*, Isaac and his *Frau*, Mercy, were to be ushers, or *Forgeher* at the wedding, along with two other couples.

Josiah would also be there, she knew, as he was one of Gideon's *Newehockers*. Not seated in the back of the room where she might be able to ignore him, but right at the front as one of Gideon's wedding attendants.

For a moment she felt betrayed by her *Onkle* for asking Josiah to do this and then she sent up a prayer, asking for forgiveness. Gideon had the right to ask whoever he chose to be his attendants. Just because she was all twisted up inside about Josiah didn't mean her *Onkle* couldn't ask him to have a role at the wedding.

In the hours ahead, she chattered with the other women and kept her gaze lowered as Gideon's friends found their way into the Hershberger kitchen for their early breakfast.

"Are you okay?" Sarah whispered from her position beside Leah, waiting to ladle gravy over the biscuits she gave out to the *Menner*. "I hope you're not sickening…today of all days."

"I'm fine," she responded shortly, growing warm as Josiah filed past to collect his biscuit.

"I hope so," the *Maedel* next to her said. "These two will be very happy, I think."

"*Yah*. They will."

Even though she hadn't looked up, she somehow knew when Josiah stood in front of her.

"*Goedemorgen*, Leah."

Josiah's voice was as familiar as the sound of her own breathing. Without looking up, Leah murmured, "*Goedemorgen*."

Her heart thundering, her peripheral vision told her that, after a moment, the *Mann* in front of her moved away. Why could she not make up her mind about him?

Later that morning, after the church members had sung hymns while the bishop counseled Gideon and Hagar privately, the pair came into the main room and sat down—*Newehockers* beside them—for the sermon that would follow.

Leah sat, several chairs away from Josiah, as Bishop Yoder's words flowed over and around her.

As much as she tried to focus on his sermon, her mind kept returning to her own situation. She was tired of thinking about it and that seemed like all she could do these days.

As the room heated from all the bodies there, her gaze rested on Hagar and Gideon. The two had disliked one another so long, for years, it seemed. At least, Hagar had disliked Gideon a lot. Her *Onkle* was a sociable *Mann* and got along well with most everyone, but he and Hagar had a difficult past.

Leah contemplated the pair, musing on their difficult journey. This day had seemed farfetched. Her friend had been so upset when her *Mamm*, Esther, had deeded the blacksmith forge in the yard behind this very *Haus* to Gideon after Hagar's hardworking *Daed* passed away.

Staring at the couple, Leah found herself wondering if…if maybe her own journey could have such a happy outcome. Could she and Josiah find a way to one another?

She admitted to herself that she ached for this.

He'd looked so earnest when he proposed to her this time, so genuine.

Feeling her insides go mushy as she remembered the moment, Leah lifted her gaze to him. He looked…sad…and a little heart sore. Leah realized that she didn't want him to feel rebuffed by her.

She loved him.

Leah's heart constricted in her chest. She could be standing at the front, promising to love Josiah.

Maybe he'd meant what he'd said to her. Maybe he was ready to be a husband and a *Daed*...

She loved him.

At that moment, it all came clear to her. Accepting Josiah's proposal seemed the right...the best...thing to do. He'd said he was changed.

The sermon concluding, Bishop Troyer asked Gideon and Hagar to step forward.

Listening as the bishop began questioning them about their marriage, Leah felt her eyes dampen when each spoke vows of love and faithfulness. The bishop then blessed their union before several older *Menner* in the congregation began testifying about marriage.

If Gideon and Hagar's fathers were still with them, they'd have spoken first at that point. When the *Menner* were finished, the bishop offered a prayer and the wedding was over.

At this point, all the women headed toward the kitchen to begin serving a meal to the crowd, Leah rose to go help, aware that several of the younger *Maedels* were gathering excitedly around Hagar.

Involuntarily, Leah's stare followed Josiah as he threaded his way through the chattering girls toward the back of the room.

Gazing after him, her heart froze as she saw to whom he made such a beeline.

Ada Miller sat at the back of the room, her white *Kapp* neat on her smooth, blonde hair, her expression as distant and cool as Leah remembered. Josiah's *Mamm* was here. How had she forgotten?

His chilly, always polite, perfect *Mamm*, prettier than any other older woman Leah knew.

Swallowing hard against the sudden bitter taste in her mouth, she couldn't tear her gaze away.

Of course, he'd go to his *Mamm*, the woman he always put first.

159

Chapter Twelve

Ada
<u>Mannheim</u>

Ada sat back against a wall in the Hershberger *Haus* in a chair Josiah had found her, the wedding having just finished. Fanning herself as she looked around at those crowded into the *Haus*, she let their chatter flow over her. The couple being married had looked sweet and intense when they answered the minister's questions.

Although she couldn't see much of the *Newehockers* from her seat at the back of the room, she'd noted how often her Josiah had looked over at a certain *Maedel* in a black *Kapp* who was seated next to the blue-gowned bride.

This must be Leah and Ada had studied the girl's profile several times during the sermon. She was an uncommonly pretty girl, not that the outside was as important as the heart

The *Maedel* who had made Josiah forget himself and the teachings of his youth so completely that he'd made a child with her outside of marriage. Josiah wasn't a *Mann* to be foolishly led into temptation, however, Ada knew he usually did what he believed was best. He was stern in doing the right thing, but he lost his head with his Leah.

A mother wanted a girl for her son who would help him live a godly life, but Ada recognized that Josiah tended to be—like her—a little removed, a little contained. If Leah brought him out of that, she just might help him grow even closer to *Gott*.

And there was a child of their union!

With lots of movement around her, she held her place. Mothers led their *Kinder* to the kitchen to get food for hungry mouths and Ada watched from a distance, seeing Leah out at a table, serving soup.

Her heart melting within her, Ada thought about Josiah's *Boppli*. She could hardly wait to meet Leah and the child.

What a *Maedel*! So young and so staunch. *Yah*, she'd taken wrong steps, but all made mistakes and *Gott* loved them still.

Mistakes brought challenges and sometimes hard learning. When Ada thought of all Leah had faced and faced alone…

Looking around the room with as much casualness as she could muster, she searched for the many small *Buwe's* for one with Josiah's—and her poor dead Seth's—features. There were many, many families in the room and several filed past her as they went to get meals from the kitchen. Although she searched the faces she could see, none seemed particularly familiar.

Swinging back, she stared at Leah again.

Fair and lovely, Josiah had said about her, like the smitten *Buwe* he was.

How had Ada not seen this in him?

*

Leah
Mannheim

Reminding herself—and failing to listen to her own reminders—Leah kept tearing her gaze off Josiah. As she moved among the crowd attending Gideon and Hagar's wedding, she served out scoops of green beans with an absent smile, some weird sense keeping her informed as to his location in the gathering. Somehow, she managed her job while her awareness was shamefully honed in on the one *Mann* she should ignore.

Leah wanted to cry, but she kept a smile plastered on her face.

Josiah had more than indicated his loyalties by racing off to his *Mamm's* side as soon as he could. Her vision blurred with tears and she forced a wider smile on her face, telling herself that some hearts never mended and she needed to get on with raising her son.

"Here you go, *Frau* Bontrager," she murmured, serving a woman not much older who sat with two small *Dochders*.

"*Denki*," the mother responded. "As soon as I feed these two, Leah, I'll join you in the kitchen."

"No problem." She forced another smile. "Whenever you can."

161

Moving on down the row, she served another *familye*, this with seven *Kinder* of different sizes.

Turning to start down the next row of tables, she found herself face-to-face with Josiah Miller. Until that moment, she been too distracted by her own rigid focus on the task at hand and hadn't realized he'd left the back of the room.

Time seemed to spin to a stop as she stared into his face. When the moment passed and she drew a breath, trying to settle herself, Leah looked over his shoulder and got another shock.

Just behind Josiah was Ada Miller, the white *Kapp* on her head starched and smooth, a small smile widening her mouth. In all her time in Windber, Leah had never seen the calm and collected *Frau* Miller look as genuinely warm. The woman was always pleasant and nice enough, in a general social way, but never all that welcoming. Standing slightly behind her son in the crowded room, she met Leah's eyes with a slight, but friendly smile.

"Stop a moment," Josiah said to Leah abruptly, his expression tense, but determined. "Leah, this is my *Mamm*. I want you to meet Ada Miller. *Mamm*, this is Leah, who I told you about."

His voice strong, he added, "The girl I love."

Staring at him in complete shock, Leah's mouth dropped open. This was beyond weird. Emotional public declarations weren't made in their community. That sober Josiah would say this startled her even more.

The older woman reached her hand forward to Leah, a cautious smile on her face, as if she were…nervous, a thing Leah couldn't have even imagined.

"Leah! How nice to meet you."

To have the smooth, always-in-control *Frau* be both friendly and nervous about meeting her widened Leah's eyes. If her hand hadn't been taken in such a warm grasp, she'd wonder if she were dreaming.

Ada Miller glanced around the room. "Where are your *familye* and your little *Buwe*, Eli, sitting?"

*

162

Ada
<u>Mannheim</u>

Sitting outside the wedding *Haus* later at a table a little removed from the groups of chattering friends around her, Ada felt limp from those few moments with Leah's *familye* and Josiah's *Boppli*. This unexpected turn of events showed a different side of her son, who had seemed shuttered and locked into himself these last few years. Now, she knew why!

Drawing in a deep breath in silence as she enjoyed a moment to collect herself, Ada watched the different clusters of friends, glad to be able to step-back.

Josiah had marched her forward with determination to meet his Leah. Even now, when matters were still unsettled, he seemed...stronger. This Leah seemed to have been *gut* for him, even though they'd had an unhappy period.

Leah had seemed shocked to meet her, although the girl had to know she was here in Mannheim. Did she think Josiah would fail to make the introduction? From what Ada could see, there were matters to be settled between them.

Lunch had finished a little while before and the women had gathered dishes to be washed. The fall air was warmer now, as the sun shone down on the yard beside the *Haus*. Golden leaves fluttered from a tall, nearby tree with every puff of breeze.

Sitting alone in a pool of quiet, it took a moment before Ada recognized the *Mann* striding toward her through the groups of visiting friends.

Luke!

She straightened in her chair. Frowning, her focus sharpened suddenly on him.

Standing to move forward to greet him, Ada tried to calm the sudden thumping of her heart. Sitting here as if she didn't see or know Luke wasn't an option, although she had a cowardly urge to ignore the whole...mess she felt.

Drawing a deep breath, she curved her mouth into a quiet, welcoming smile. Assuming her superficial, social role, she strolled to meet him, hating that remaining calm with Luke was now difficult for her.

163

He was a member of her community, nothing more! she told herself firmly, despite what Judith said.

Still, it was strange that he'd come here.

If Luke were in Mannheim, there must be a problem at the farm, Ada reasoned as she threaded her way through the clusters of people. What problem, she couldn't imagine. He'd handled many things himself, big and small. What could have happened that he'd need to consult Josiah?

"Ada," he said when they came together, the wide brim of his hat shading his lean face.

"Hello." Her heart now thundered in her ears as her thoughts began cataloging everything about him, her gaze clinging to the sight of him. His broad shoulders, encased in his dark suit, the height of him that had her looking up.

"Is there a problem on the farm?" she asked, her voice as unflustered as she could make it. "Josiah is around somewhere."

"I saw him over by the front of the *Haus*, playing with some little *Buwe*," Luke responded, his hazel stare intent of her face. "How are you?"

The question held an intimate note, a warmth she'd have sworn wasn't there six months ago.

"I'm fine, of course," she said, in a faintly-amused and dismissive voice as she tried to keep the flush from her cheeks. Having lived some years, she'd learned to recognize this kind of intent look. "The little *Buwe* you saw Josiah playing with is his son. Josiah has a son, can you imagine? He just told me, said he's loved the *Boppli's Mamm* ever since they met several years ago."

"Oh? No, I didn't know he was interested in any one *Maedel*, although I suspected that. And they have a son?" He craned around, looking back in the direction from which he'd come. "That doesn't sound like our Josiah."

"*Neh*, it doesn't," she agreed. "Apparently, he asked her to marry him years back, but they got into an argument. It's a long story."

"Sounds like," Luke looked back at her.

"An argument over me. I was the reason Josiah didn't marry her right then." Ada felt herself grow more red. "I only wanted him to find his own happiness, his own path with *Gott*, but

164

my son evidently believed I didn't know Leah well enough and they…delayed getting married."

Luke's smile faded as she said this.

"But he didn't delay in getting in the *familye* way?"

"*Neh*." She looked down and then back up. "I-I know he's worried about me. I feel responsible for all this."

A faint smile coasted over his face. "You can't be responsible for them getting in the *familye* way."

"It's nothing to joke about," she snapped, angry at herself and at him.

"*Neh*, it's not." All joking left his face." I didn't come here to speak to Josiah."

She lifted her gaze, noting that lighthearted looked more serious and determined than ever. "You didn't?"

"No." He reached out for her.

Ada jumped, but made no remark when he grasped her hand in his, wondering if her cheeks could get any redder.

"Why are you here then?" she asked in a strangled voice, frustrated that she was reacting in this moment as if she was fifteen again.

"For you," the tall *Mann* next to her said, her hand still in his. "Let's not beat about the bush, Ada. Or waste any more time. I love you and I know you love me, as well. Let's marry."

As if all the voices around her receded, she heard a buzzing in her ears and the terror she'd felt when she thought he'd fallen off the stack of hay bales returned in a flash.

"Don't be ridiculous," she replied in a waspish voice, suddenly and acutely aware of the public nature of the interaction. All around them chattered others, caught up for the moment, but they had to soon notice the two standing together like fenceposts entwined.

"We are not *Youngies* to be carried away by dreams! This is silly," she said, casting a quick glance around.

His grip tightened and she tried then to pull away. She should have done this before. Ada didn't know what she was thinking to allow Luke this familiarity. "What we feel for one another is very real. Marry me."

Ada stared at him, both reluctant to become the center of everyone's attention and lost in the words that had just spilled from him. A strange combination of fear and excitement buzzed in her head.

Gripped suddenly by a sense that she couldn't do this—couldn't risk losing a *Mann* even more precious than Abraham had been to her, she forced her lips up in an awkward, tense attempt at a smile. "You needn't do this. I am happy with Josiah's choice of *Frau*. We will do well enough."

"I don't care," he snapped, "whether or not Josiah marries his son's *Mamm*. This has nothing to do with that. I didn't even know of that when I came to get you. You and I love one another and we should marry."

Reaching for ground that had been solid beneath her feet ever since her husband died, Ada snapped back, "*Neh*. We should not marry! I have been told again and again to take another *Mann*, that this is what *Gott* decreed women should do. *Neh*, I say. I will not marry again."

"You can do this, Ada," Luke said, his voice gentling. "You've been afraid a very long time, but I know—and *Gott* knows—that you can do this. You can take this risk."

"I cannot!" she yelped, snatching her hand away from him. "I won't. I don't love you, Luke. I've never loved you."

The smile wiped from his face, Luke regarded her steadily. "*Yah. Yah*, you do. I have come here and offered you my heart and my hand. I have risked all to say this to you. It is up to you whether you marry me. I cannot make you trust and have faith. You must do this alone."

All the blood had left her face now and she said through tight lips, "I cannot."

*

Leah
Mannheim

"Now! Now you introduce me?" Leah yelped angrily, motioning Josiah vigorously to retreat with her to the back of the room.

Shocked by her reaction, he gaped at her.

166

His *Mamm* now sitting out in the yard amidst the visiting wedding attendees, Josiah had sought Leah out, thrown by her angry greeting.

Standing now at the back of the Hershberger kitchen, the door at Leah's back, he blinked and tried to understand why she was so incensed. To his bafflement, she seemed furious.

"But you wanted me to—" he started to say, "I thought you wanted me to introduce my *Mamm* to you!"

"*Yah!*" Leah whisper-yelled, "before! When we were in Windber and you asked me to marry you! I wanted you then to act as a *Mann* in love."

"I just did introduce you!" he said indignantly. "I don't understand why you're so angry."

She shook her head in exasperation, her expression irate. "Now! I don't believe you. After all this time! All this grief! Now he does this simple thing!"

Glancing around to see if their argument was attracting attention, Josiah said in a voice made annoyed by his complete confusion. "I thought you wanted me to bring my *Mamm* over. I asked you to marry me. To do this, it's only natural that you meet my mother."

He paused before adding in a strong voice. "And Eli? Of course, I told my *Mamm* I have a son!"

Leah made him crazy! He couldn't imagine being so annoyed in speaking to anyone else but her.

"If you'd loved me," she hissed with intensity, "you'd have done this long ago!"

"I do love you!" he snarled back. "I've offered marriage to you. Many times! I've been open with my *Mamm* about everything. I told her about Eli."

"I guess you want a pat on the back for that," she said waspishly. "I'm sure it was difficult to tell her."

"It was!" He felt his face getting red. "I can't imagine most *Eldre* want their sons to have *surprise* children!"

Her gaze scanning the room behind him at the women working in the kitchen, Leah grabbed him by the arm to pull Josiah out on the kitchen porch with her.

"He wouldn't have been a surprise child," she snarled when they stood outside the kitchen, "if you'd have behaved then as if you wanted to marry me!"

"I had asked you to marry!" He glanced side to side at the clusters of people in the back yard, lowering his voice. "I was never with any other woman as I was with you. Of course, I wanted to marry you."

He dropped the volume of his words even more. "Do you think I'd have ever done that if I didn't plan on marrying you? And I thought you wanted to meet my *Mamm*! I thought…that was what I should do."

Leah shook her head sorrowfully. "*What you should do*! I did want that, Josiah. I wanted it terribly—before. Why couldn't you have done that before? You would have. If you really loved me."

Scrubbing a hand across her wet cheeks, she turned away, dashing down the porch steps.

*

Early the next morning, Leah stood from the low milking stool, patting the haunch of the cow she'd just finished. She'd left her *Schweschder*, Grace, to watch Eli while she finished her chores. A cock crowed in the faint light and Leah moved on to the last in the row of cows waiting to be milked.

Despair sat in her chest like a heavy stone on her heart. It should have mattered that Josiah had introduced her to his *Mamm*. Finally. The long delay in his doing what should have been the most natural thing troubled her still.

If he'd truly loved her, wouldn't he have wanted to immediately tell his mother about her? He'd proposed in the fall that year. They could have been married just weeks later.

That's what she'd assumed would happen. Then he said he didn't want to tell anyone yet. This meant he didn't want to marry her for a whole year? Farm folk had many things to which to attend during the growing season. Marriages took place in the fall, after the heavy work on farms was finished for the year.

The fresh morning air cooled her cheeks as she stepped out of the barn a few minutes later, the milk pail sloshing in her hold.

In the hen house, Anna—just elder to Grace—was finishing feeding the chickens. Every now and then the rooster could be heard again, proclaiming the dawn.

The milk slopping against the sides of her pail, Leah started toward the kitchen only to stop in crossing the yard as a buggy pull up in front of the *Haus*.

To her shock, Ada Miller sat behind the buggy horse, alone on the box. The wheat-fair hair beneath her neat white *Kapp* seemed, in the growing morning light, to be free of even faint threads of silver.

Leah's milk bucket settled on the dewy ground with a thud as she stood, suddenly rooted in place in the middle of the yard.

Ada Miller was here at the Lapp farm? So early in the morning, this couldn't be a casual call.

Seeing Josiah's mother here made Leah's mouth feel dry, as if the schoolteacher had asked her a question to which she didn't have an answer.

The older woman capably secured the buggy horse's reins before descending from the buggy with a youthful nimbleness that didn't even surprise Leah. Josiah's mother seemed graceful and energetic in every way, way too young to have a grown son.

"Leah Lapp!" Ada called across the short distance. "Can we talk?"

Her chest tight with dread and questions, Leah opened her mouth to answer, suddenly aware that Anna had appeared beside her, hissing, "What is she doing here?"

"I have no idea," Leah responded through numb lips.

"Well," her sister grabbed Leah's pail, nudging her forward. "Go ahead. Talk to her. I'll take the milk inside."

Sparing her *Schweschder* a quick glance of gratitude, Leah turned toward Josiah's slender, formidable *Mamm*, reminding herself that she had no reason to shrink from this confrontation. Not really. She hadn't forced Josiah into making Eli.

She walked forward, meeting Ada with a forced, welcoming smile. No doubt reproaches would follow, but that was no reason not to be kind and receptive. This is what *Gott* would expect of her.

169

As they came together, Ada said, "I'm very sorry. This is all my fault, Leah. All my fault. Please forgive me. Please don't hold this against Josiah."

Looking up with a grimace, she added, "Although Josiah has been a fool."

Surprised by this opening, Leah's mouth dropped open and she had to snap it shut. She'd expected the older woman to have insisted her son was a very desirable marriage partner and to rag at Leah for not marrying him immediately. She expected the woman to have chastised Leah for everything.

"What?"

Ada's mouth worked a moment. "Josiah told me…everything. His reasons for doing what he did. His mistakes."

Leah stared at the woman, the attractive face under her *Kapp* seemed older suddenly, tired and even more mask-like.

Josiah's mother looked down. "I'm—I've never been very good with—with people I don't know well."

She lifted her gaze to meet Leah's. "I know I can seem cold. Disinterested, even. I don't mean to. Josiah means the world to me. I want him to be happy and I realize I've—I've gotten in his way. I'm sorry for causing you both grief."

As if she were paralyzed, Leah couldn't think of a thing to say…although she suddenly felt an unexpected urge to comfort Ada Miller. In a weird flash, she got the impression that Ada was owning this as much for her own sake as for her son's.

"Josiah has always tried to…protect me," Ada said. "After his *Daed* and *Bruder* died when he was just a little *Buwe*, he kept…patting me and telling me everything would work out. He even said they were just gone for a little while and would soon come home."

Ada's mouth worked a moment, her eyes growing wet. "A little *Buwe*, trying to comfort his *Mamm*."

A sympathetic murmur escaped Leah.

Ada nodded decisively, as if trying step out of herself. She wiped a hand across her cheek, saying. "Can you imagine? I was the *Mamm* and he felt the need to care for me. Anyway, as you can imagine, he and I have always been very close. Almost a pair against the world, although many others helped us, of course. Luke came soon after Abe's death and he's—he's been very helpful to Josiah. Keeping the farm going."

"That must have been a big relief," Leah said, finally finding her voice. "I'm sure his *Daed* would have wanted that."

"*Yah*," the older woman agreed. "He was the best and kindest *Mann*."

Their surroundings sinking into the background, Leah huddled her sweater around herself in the chilly air, knowing she'd rather freeze to death than break this moment.

"I came here to see you," Ada said, "because I see now that, in my love for Josiah and—and my fear of losing again—I've held him too close. I've stopped moving forward because I thought that would keep me from that loss again, but—"

She stopped, looking directly into Leah's face. "—but I didn't realize I was keeping Josiah from moving forward, too."

Taking a deep breath, she reached her hand out with that same look of determination.

Leah grasped it automatically, feeling giddy from the sharp turn from anxiety to unexpected relief that the conversation brought. The other woman's hand felt colder and smaller than hers. Somehow, she seemed...frailer than Leah would have expected.

"Josiah loves you, Leah," Ada continued, her voice growing stronger.

Without meaning to, Leah made a sound of denial.

Moving on as if the younger woman had said nothing, Ada continued "—After the two of you spoke at the wedding yesterday, he was very upset. He told me everything—all that he hadn't said before—and he is upset that he hadn't told me before. I know I have held him too close, but, yesterday, he made it clear that this is at an end. He actually bade me not to stick my nose in where it didn't belong."

She hiccupped a little laugh. "He even told me I should find myself a husband. Said he's seen men smile at me with interest."

Rolling her eyes, she continued, "Such a silly *Buwe*, he spoke of several that he called fine, including our farm manager!"

A rush of emotion choking her, Leah impulsively squeezed the hand in hers, feeling warmer toward the older woman than

171

she'd ever thought possible. She smiled, saying, "I think he's right, Ada. You should take a husband, maybe smile back at one or two of those men."

"Maybe." Ada's damp chuckle was faint. "You should know that Josiah's coming here to see you today."

Leah's smile faded. "Today?"

"*Yah*," nodded Ada. "He said he loves you and will keep telling you until you believe him."

"Maybe," Leah said, her thoughts whirling in her head, "Maybe."

*

Ada
<u>Mannheim</u>

The sun now solidly set higher in the blue, fall sky, Ada reflected that she'd never been good at groveling, even as a child when one naturally got used to others knowing better. Still, she had to find Luke.

Drawing her buggy into the row of others parked at Bontreger's store later that same morning, she tied the reins and climbed down.

Luke was here, her son told her, making a stop before heading back to Windber after traveling here to tell her of his love.

Ada's eyes blurred over again. Out of her fear, she'd rejected him yesterday and she had to find him before he left.

She had to.

Her ruminations on the way back from Leah's home had led Ada to this one conviction. No one—not one *Mann*—had ever dented her awareness after her husband died. Not one, until Luke.

Broad shouldered and strong, fighting through rain and drought, he'd always been there. Somehow through the years of working along one's side to keep Josiah's farm running, Luke had wiggled his way into her heart without her noticing.

Laughing, joking Luke. So different from Abraham, different to from the sober woman she'd become. He—he'd made her laugh, made her comfortable. Made her uncomfortable.

She had to find him.

Looking at the bustling store, Ada knew she had to unsay everything she'd said when he laid his heart before her.

The store looked full of customers, as when she'd had her big conversation with Hagar Hershberger that day when here with Josiah, and Sapphira Schwartz, the matchmaker.

There couldn't be a more public place to meet Luke, but she had to make him hear how much she loved him. She could not let him return to Windber without telling him how she really felt. If she had to grovel and beg him to let her change her mind, then that was what she had to do..

Her mouth felt dry and dusty at the thought of—of both taking and not taking this risk. Yet, she knew she wouldn't have had such a big reaction to thinking he was dead, mangled at the bottom of the pile of bales, if she hadn't already come to losing her heart to him.

No question of taking a risk to love him, she'd already let him in.

Pushing open the door, the chatter of gossiping folk hit her like a strong wind. People everywhere, all seeming to suddenly be staring her way. Suddenly, it was very hot. She stepped inside and stopped, her heart seeming to have risen into her throat.

There he was. At the register, talking to the storekeeper with no smile on Luke's face. She'd never once seen Luke looking so somber.

"I'll take just this—"

Before she could think, she called out, "Luke!"

Looking around at her cry, his mouth opened when he saw Ada there, as if to respond.

Her heart beat faster at the welcome in his face. Then, the light went out of his eyes, his expression hardening, and he turned back to the *Mann* behind the counter.

The noise in the store jolted again to a noisy babble, as if those around them were covering up the awkward moment.

Riddled with uncertainty and profoundly aware of surreptitious stares centered on her, she didn't move from the door.

Maybe he hated her now. The thought streaked past along with a conviction that she'd messed things up this time. Some were like that, their hearts like a slammed door. Then, Ada's

173

mouth thinned and her jaw set. Regardless of everything, she had to somehow make him listen.

Stubborn *Mann.*

No matter how much he didn't want to talk to her, she wasn't moving. He had to come this way to get to his buggy. She planted herself in his path. She wouldn't have chosen to speak in this public place, but she couldn't let him leave.

A bag of apples in one hand, he left the register, walking her way.

"I must speak to you, Luke," she said when he got close. Ada tried not to tremble. She never showed weakness, no matter how weak she felt, she reminded herself.

"May I pass, please?" he asked in an unyielding voice, polite but still grim.

Very aware of their confrontation having become the center of attention, she flushed, but refused to let her embarrassment take over. Ada lifted her chin, repeating, "I must talk with you."

Luke looked at her a moment without his usual grin. "Okay."

Glancing around the store, she saw that it seemed every eye was focused on them. Ada swallowed and then stubbornly thrust her jaw forward.

He would listen to her.

A smile tugged at the corner of his mouth, the big Mann standing before her.

A hush had fallen over the previously noisy store. His grin widening, he looked around at the avid crowd and then back at her before nodding toward the door.

Ada drew a breath of relief. He clearly expected her to precede him.

Turning with appreciation, she quickly went out to the porch in front of the building. He could have unkindly made her grovel in a very public way.

A fall breeze tugged at her skirt and cooled her off as she stepped onto the porch. Ada paused, knowing a rocky road still lie ahead.

"I'm sorry." The words popped out as they descended the steps.

He glanced over. "What? What for?"

"That I said what I did yesterday." Ada knew she had to make her feelings known to him.

"A woman has a right to say what she wants." He looked down, a muscle working in his lean cheek. A social *Mann*, she'd never seen Luke this terse.

She hurriedly said, "But I didn't—not really. Say what I want, I mean."

A pair of women passed them on their way inside the store, throwing curious looks their way. Despite their keen audience when inside the store, it was the Amish way to mind their own business and not intrude into others' matters, but the conversation she and Luke had to look...intense.

"Can we walk toward your buggy?" Ada whispered.

He glanced over, as if just noticing these new observers. "Sure."

They moved toward Luke's buggy under a fringe of trees at the side of the lot.

He turned toward her, the store behind him. "Now, what? What do you mean? Not really?"

"I didn't really say what I wanted," Ada blurted out. She was a mature *Frau*. She hadn't blurted anything out for years, but she felt awkward now and giddy enough to be sick. Even when Abraham asked her to be his wife, she hadn't felt this way.

"You seemed very clear," Luke said in a level, non-Luke voice.

"I didn't—didn't speak the truth. I was afraid!" She blinked to clear her vision. "I've been...afraid, been protecting myself...for so long. I think I even blocked out *Gott's* voice."

Luke waited for her to continue.

Looking down to where she held her hands, clasped together to keep them from shaking, Ada said, "You—you mean a lot to me, Luke. More than—more than anyone has, besides Josiah, and that scared me. Scares me. I nearly lost my mind when I thought you'd fallen off the stack of hay bales!"

"I'm sorry about that," he said quickly. "I was just playing and I had no idea of upsetting you."

Taking a step toward him, she leaned out to clutch the narrow lapel of his jacket, the heat of him welcome against her knuckles. "Don't you see? I don't think I'd have had that reaction, been that upset, if—if I didn't—care for you."

Having gone still at her touch, he'd lowered his gaze to where she held his jacket. "Care for me?"

Dropping her voice to a whisper, Ada said, "You told me... When you came to the wedding yesterday...you loved me. That you knew I loved you."

"*Yah.*"

Throwing her head back now, she added tartly, "And don't forget you were the first to say I'd held Josiah too close."

"I was, wasn't I?" A thread of self-congratulatory humor ran through his words.

"Well, you were right." Feeling herself flush, she admitted to what she'd done. "In my own holding him that close, I—I didn't do either of us a favor."

"Are you?" he paused. "Are you saying that you do...love me?"

"Yes! But don't let it go to your head, Luke Fisher. You're not right all the time!"

He laughed, gathering her into his arms. "It's enough, dear Ada, to have been right this time."

Moments later, she emerged from his ruthless kiss, catching her breath. Blinking up at him, all she could say was, "Oh!"

"I love you. I love you." He kissed her again. "If you'll marry me, I'll promise before *Gott* to never again to pretend to fall off a stack of hay bales. I'll never again give you a reason to be afraid."

Looking up into his face, Ada smiled, saying ruefully, "Yes, you will...but I will pray that *Gott* give me the strength to keep risking with you."

*

Leah
Mannheim

Later that same day, Leah sat on a chair, shelling peas under a tree behind the *Haus*. Her *Mamm* sat beside her engaged in the same occupation while little Eli toddled around them, chasing a ladybug.

Ever since the morning visit from Josiah's mother, Leah had wrestled with a web of thoughts—maybe Josiah really did love her… His mother thought so. Could Leah trust him? Maybe he meant that he wanted to cherish her all their lives…although that seemed unlikely given what he'd said about his *Mamm*. Maybe he was just following his mother's directions to marry Leah to bring his son into his *Haus*.

Then again, maybe he did love her.

Around and round her thoughts went until she felt crazy.

As the procession of thoughts tromped through her head, she looked up to see a sandy-haired *Mann* in a broad-brimmed hat come round the corner of her *Haus*.

Leah reached out, gripping her *Mamm's* arm. Rachel had heard all about Ada's early visit and her statement that Josiah would come that day.

Her heart beating faster, a tumble of emotion ran through Leah.

"*Frau* Lapp," Josiah greeted her mother when he got close to their shady spot under the tree.

"*Goedemorgen*," Rachel smiled at him. Looking at her flushed *Dochder*, she said, "Leah, why don't I take Eli in for a nap?"

At Leah's unintelligible response, she moved off to scoop up the protesting *Buwe* and disappear into the *Haus*.

"I've not come to distress you," he said after her *Mamm* had left. Standing in front of her in the shadow of the spreading tree, he slipped off his broad brimmed hat, his face serious.

Yellow leaves from the branches above occasionally drifted down with puffs of breeze, scattering on the ground beneath the tree.

"I don't know what to say," she responded after a minute, her stomach in knots. She knew she should sacrifice her own happiness for her son to be raised as other *Kinner*. She'd already deserted him once. Eli was loved, happy, safe and fed here…but

177

he didn't have a *Daed* of his own. He was being raised as a fatherless *Buwe*, like Josiah.

"Just listen to me," Josiah begged.

Stiffening and trying to be strong in this, she looked at him. *Gott* wanted her to be loved, to be happy. She had lost her heart to Josiah, but she didn't know if she could be his *Frau*, lay by his side at night, knowing he didn't love her.

And yet she should do finally what was best for her little boy. She just didn't know what to do. It felt as if she were being torn apart inside.

Josiah's throat constricted visibly. "I will not press you, Leah. Not anymore. I want—I still want—you and Eli to live with me. I want to marry you...but more than that, I want you happy."

Confused, she stared at him.

He took his hat off, hitting it against his knee. "I'm making a mess of this, I know. I just came today to reassure you that I will be Eli's *Daed*, regardless. You don't have the marry me for me to do this. I will come here to Mannheim every year whenever my farm doesn't need me. I will make sure he knows he has a *Daed* who loves him, but I will not try to force you to do anything."

Saying this, he looked up, his cheeks flushed as he met her gaze.

Leah started crying, burying her face in her hand. His words should have been a relief. Her son would know his father. Her tears didn't stop, though, noisy sobs erupting to her dismay. She turned her face away, not able to bear that he witnessed her break down.

Josiah didn't love her. His words were an admission of this.

Taking a quick step forward when she began crying in earnest, he dropped to his knees in front of her, his hat now cast aside. Reaching out to cover the hand in her lap with his, he urged her, "Don't! Don't cry, my Leah. I understand that my—my actions may have killed your caring for me, but I mean not to worry you about this anymore."

As she sat on her chair under the spreading, faded tree—the fall wind drifting by in gusts—they were alone in this place of her childhood, wrestling with this very grown up situation.

"Please don't cry," he repeated.

The tenderness in his voice made her cry harder, though. She'd so long to hear this note in his words again, to find this Josiah, the one with which she'd fallen in love. It was almost too precious to believe. Was she asleep and dreaming this?

"You don't have to worry." He assured her. "I promise this. I won't pressure you again. You don't want—for whatever reason—to marry me and I can't accept that. I'll—I'll try to accept that. I just want you to know that I want you to be happy. This is your decision, Leah. I love you and I love Eli, but I won't have you forced into anything."

Pausing, he said with a despairing note in his voice, "I love you too much for that. I've told my *Mamm* about you and our son. I should have done this long ago—not that I knew then about Eli—but I've told her, too, to stop searching for a wife for me."

Dropping the hand she'd had covering her eyes, Leah stared at him, her vision wavering through the tears that lingered there.

"I don't want another wife," he said earnestly. "Only you, but as that's not happening, I accept your choice. You must do what you think best. I will live with this. Loving you, I will live with this."

"You'd do this...for me?" Her heart quickening, she asked the question through numb lips. "You'd give up? Accept that I may marry another and that your son would grow up in our *Haus*? Why? Why are you promising this?"

"Because I love you!" he said, his voice sounding almost angry in his intensity. His hand tightening over hers, he repeated, "I love you. I see now that I was young and foolish—an idiot—when I wanted you to wait to marry. I should have marched into my *Mamm* right then and presented you to her! I should have married you as quickly as I could. We had—had already made Eli, although we didn't know it. Already started our *familye*. I guess I was scared, confused about being a *Mann*. I don't know, but I'd do it all differently, if I could."

"You're saying...that you won't take Eli away? You'd leave him to me to raise?"

A muscle in his jaw worked. "*Yah*, but I will be his *Daed*. It will take some explaining, at some point, but, *yah*, you—you

179

don't have to marry me. I accept that I messed everything up two years ago. I should have scooped you up and married you then."

"You do love me!" she breathed, a crushing weight lifting off her. He'd stayed to help her injured *Daed* bring in the farm's crops, even though he had crops of his own to concern him. Accepted her help even when she was laughing at him.

He'd finally chosen her first, before even his *Mamm* and now he was sacrificing his own desires for her. Although he wanted her and his son under his own roof, he was accepting her right to decide her own future.

He—he loved her! Leah sat stunned as the realization spread through her.

"*Yah*," he said, "I do. As I've told you, I'm marrying no one else. Only you, if you'll have me. If not, I'll—I guess I'll be alone."

"Oh, Josiah!" Her wavering smile breaking through, she reached for his hand. "You love me! If—if you really love me and place me in a *Frau's* place, I—I am so relieved!"

Not waiting for the last word to leave her mouth, Josiah pulled her to her feet and folded her tightly in his arms.

"Don't toy with me, Leah," he said in a shaking voice a few minutes later. "I'll give in to my worst instincts and throw you over my knee before spanking you. Don't tease me about this. My feelings will get the better of me."

Her hand crept up to stroke his jaw and she said in a laughing voice, as shaken as his, "You'd do that? If I teased you?"

"I might," Josiah pulled her tighter, "I've tried everything else."

"Don't worry," she said, her words loving. "Your *Frau* will keep you in line."

*****

Thank You!

Thanks so much for purchasing Amish Prodigal! If you enjoyed this book, please consider leaving a review at **XXXXX** and watch for Amish Rogue, Book 6, the last in the series! Authors live and die by reviews and I would be very grateful if you would do me the honor of leaving one. Thanks in advance. I so appreciate it!

Please watch for Amish Rogue (Amish Vows Romance, Bk 6), which tells Sarah Beiler and Mark Fisher's story—Upcoming soon!

****

Freebie Alert!

Did you enjoy Leah and Josiah's story? A Prequel to Amish Renegade (Amish Vows romance, Book 1) is available for free! If you liked reading Kate and Enoch's story of love rediscovered, you might like to see the parents who raised Kate and get an understanding of the foundations to her view of the world. See how her *Englischer* mother, Elizabeth, decided to leave that world and everything she's known to be with Kate's dad, James? Read for free about the struggle these two faced and how God helped them to find what they longed for. Click this link for the prequel, Amish By Choice. https://dl.bookfunnel.com/g1f5sp44gz

***

Let's Connect!

I love to hear from readers, so don't be shy, please say hello. Most days I can be found chatting about all things Amish at the links below:

Email: Rose@rosedoss.com
Website: www.rosedoss.com
Facebook: https://www.facebook.com/RoseDossBooks /
Instagram: https://www.instagram.com/rosedoss1001 /

Check out my author page https://www.amazon.com/Rose-Doss/e/B07DF7MSM2/ on Amazon to see my other books:

If you would like to be notified of new releases, free giveaways and secret bonuses click HERE https://mailchi.mp/ef2597c3d73d/win-a-free-amish-novel to join my mailing list.

About the Author

Rose Doss is an award-winning romance author. She has written twenty-eight romance novels. Her books have won numerous awards, including a final in the prestigious Romance Writers of America Golden Heart Award.

A frequent speaker at writers' groups and conferences, she has taught workshops on characterization and, creating and resolving conflict. She works full time as a therapist.

Her husband and she married when she was only nineteen and he was barely twenty-one, proving that early marriage can make it, but only if you're really lucky and persistent. They went through college and grad school together. She not only loves him still, all these years later, she still likes him—which she says is sometimes harder. They have two funny, intelligent and highly accomplished daughters. Rose loves writing and hopes you enjoy reading her work.

Amish Romances:

Amish By Choice (Amish Vows Romance, Prequel) https://dl.bookfunnel.com/g1f5sp44gz
Amish Renegade(Amish Vows Romance, Bk 1)
Amish Princess(Amish Vows Romance, Bk 2)**(insert link)**
Amish Heartbreaker(Amish Vows Romance, Bk 3)**(Insert link)**
Amish Spinster(Amish Vows Romance, Bk 4)**(Insert link)**
Amish Prodigal (Amish Vows Romance, Bk 5)**(Insert link)**
Amish Rogue(Amish Vows Romance, BK 6)—Upcoming later this year!

****

Glossary of Amish Terms:

Aenti—Aunt
Baremlich--terrible
Bencil or Bensel—silly child
Boppli—baby
Bopplin—babies
Bruder—Brother
Budder--butter
Buwe—boy
Daed—dad
Debiel—moron
Denki—Thank you
der Suh—my son
der Vedder—my father
Dochder—daughter
Dumm hund—dumb dog
Eldre—parents
Englischer—non-Amish
Fernhoodle—puzzled or perplexed
Forgeher—married couples who serve as wedding ushers
Frau—wife
Geschwischder—brothers and sisters
Goedenacht—goodnight
Goedenavond—good evening
Goedemorgen—good morning or good day
Gott—God
Grank—sick
Grossdaddi—grandfather
Grossie—big
Grossmammi—Grandmother
Gut—good
Hallo—hello
Haus—house
Hundli—Puppy
Kapp—starched white cap married females wear, black if unmarried

184

Keavlin—Diaper or supply bag for babies
Kinder or Kinner—children
Kinskind--grandchildren
Kleinzoon—grandson
Lappich buwe—silly boy
Liebling—sweetheart, darling, honey
Maedel—girl
Mamm—mom
Mann—man
Menner—Men
Narrish—crazy
Neh—No
Newehockers—Attendants at an Amish wedding
Nibling—one's siblings children
Onkle—uncle
Ordnung—the collection of regulations that govern Amish practices and behavior within a
district
Rumspringa—literally "running around", used in reference to the period when Amish youth are
given more freedom so that they can make an informed decision about being baptized into the
Amish church.
Sauer—sour
Schmaert—smart
Schaviut—rascal
Schlang—snake
Scholar—young, school-aged person
Schweschder—sister
Verhaddelt—mixed up
Verrickt—crazy
Windle—diaper
Wunderbarr or Wunderbaar—wonderful
Yah—yes
Youngies—adolescents. Young people.

Made in the USA
Monee, IL
26 February 2021

61442115R00111